D0037443

A Novel

Jonas Karlsson

Translated from the Swedish by Neil Smith

HOGARTH

London/New York

This is a work of fiction. Names, characters, places, and incidents either are the product of the author's imagination or are used fictitiously. Any resemblance to actual persons, living or dead, events, or locales is entirely coincidental.

Translation copyright © 2015 by Neil Smith

Reading Group Guide © 2015 by Random House LLC

All rights reserved.

Published in the United States by Hogarth,
an imprint of the Crown Publishing Group,
a division of Random House LLC,
a Penguin Random House Company, New York.
www.crownpublishing.com

HOGARTH is a trademark of the Random House Group Limited, and the
H colophon is a trademark of Random House LLC.
Originally published in Sweden as "Rummet" in the collection *Den Perfekta Vannen,* published by Wahlstrom & Widstrand, Stockholm, in 2009. Copyright © 2009 by Jonas Karlsson. This translation simultaneously published in the United Kingdom by Hogarth, an imprint of Chatto & Windus, a division of the Random House Group Ltd., London.
Published by agreement with the Salomonsson Agency.

Library of Congress Cataloging-in-Publication Data
Karlsson, Jonas, 1971–
  [Rummet. English]
  The room : a novel / Jonas Karlsson.—First edition.
      pages cm
1. Office workers Fiction. 2. Conformity—Fiction. 3. Psychological fiction.
I. Title.
PT9877.21.A74R8613 2014
839.73'8—dc23
2014014601

ISBN 978-0-8041-3998-4
eBook ISBN 978-0-8041-3999-1

Printed in the United States of America

Jacket design by Christopher Brand
Jacket photography by George Baier

10 9 8 7 6 5 4 3 2 1

First Edition

TO HANNA

1.

The first time I walked into the room I turned back almost at once. I was actually trying to find the toilet but got the wrong door. A musty smell hit me when I opened the door, but I don't remember thinking much about it. I hadn't actually noticed there was anything at all along this corridor leading to the lifts, apart from the toilets. Oh, I thought. A room.

I opened the door, then shut it. No more than that.

2.

I had started work at the Authority two weeks before, and in many respects I was still a newcomer. Even so, I tried to ask as few questions as I could. I wanted to become a person to be reckoned with as quickly as possible.

I had gotten used to being one of the leaders in my last job. Not a boss, or even a team manager, but someone who could sometimes show other people what to do. Not always liked, not a sycophant or a yes-man, but well regarded and treated with a certain respect, possibly even admiration. Ever so slightly ingratiating, perhaps? I was determined to build up the same position at my new place of work as soon as I could.

It wasn't really my decision to move on. I was fairly happy at my last job and felt comfortable with the routines, but somehow I outgrew the position and ended up feeling that I was doing a job that was way below my abilities, and I have to admit that I didn't always see eye to eye with my colleagues.

Eventually my former boss came and put his arm round my shoulders and told me it was time to look for a better solution. He wondered if it wasn't time for me to make a move? Move on, as he put it, gesturing upward with his hand to indicate my career trajectory. Together we went through various alternatives.

After a period of consideration and reflection I decided, in consultation with my former boss, upon the big new Authority, and after a certain amount of discussion with them it turned out that a transfer could be arranged without any great difficulty. The union agreed to it, and didn't put the brakes on like they so often do. My former boss and I celebrated with a glass of nonalcoholic cider in his office, and he wished me good luck.

The same day the first snow fell on Stockholm, I carried my boxes up the flight of steps and into the entrance of the large, redbrick building. The woman in reception smiled. I liked her at once. There was something about her manner. I knew straightaway that I had come to the right place. I straightened my back as the words "man of the future" ran through my head. A chance, I thought. Finally I would be able to blossom to my full potential. Become the person I've always wanted to be.

The new job was no better paid. Quite the opposite, in fact, it was actually slightly worse in terms of perks like flextime and vacation. And I was forced to share a desk in the middle of an open-plan office with no screens. In spite of this, I was full of enthusiasm and a desire to make a personal platform for myself and show what I was capable of from the start.

I worked out a personal strategic framework. I arrived half an hour early each morning and followed my own timetable for the day: fifty-five minutes of concentrated work, then a five-minute break, including toilet breaks. I avoided any unnecessary socializing along the way. I requested and took home files documenting previous policy decisions so as to be able to study which phrases recurred, and formed the basic vocabulary, so to speak. I spent evenings and weekends studying various structures and investigating the informal communication networks that existed within the department.

All this so that I could quickly and efficiently catch up and create a small but decisive advantage over my colleagues, who were already familiar with our workplace and the pervading conditions.

3.

I shared my desk with Håkan, who had sideburns and dark rings under his eyes. Håkan helped me with various practical details. Showed me round, gave me pamphlets, and e-mailed over documents containing all manner of information. It was presumably a welcome break from work, a chance to escape his duties, because he was always coming up with new things that he thought I ought to know about. They might be to do with the job, our colleagues, or decent places to have lunch nearby. After a while I felt obliged to point out to him that I had to be allowed to get on with my work without interruption.

"Calm down," I told him when he turned up with yet another folder, trying to get my attention. "Can you just calm down a bit?"

He calmed down at once and became considerably more reserved. Presumably sulking because I had made my feelings plain from the outset. It probably didn't sit well with the accepted image of a newcomer, but it fit with the reputation for ambition and tough tactics that I was happy to help spread about myself.

. . .

Slowly but surely I built up profiles of my closest neighbors, their character and place in the hierarchy. Beyond Håkan sat Ann. A woman somewhere round fifty. She seemed knowledgeable and ambitious, but also the sort of person who thought she knew everything and liked being proven right. It soon became clear that everyone turned to her when they didn't dare approach the boss.

She had a framed child's drawing near her computer. It showed a sun sinking into the sea. But the drawing was wrong, because on the horizon there were landmasses sticking up on both sides of the sun, which of course is impossible. Presumably it had some sort of sentimental value to her, even if it wasn't particularly pleasant for the rest of us to have to look at.

Opposite Ann sat Jörgen. Big and strong, but doubtless not possessed of an intellect to match. Pinned up on his desk and stuck all round his computer were loads of jokey notes and postcards which obviously had nothing to do with work, and suggested a tendency toward the banal. At regular intervals he would whisper things to Ann and I would hear her squeak, "Oh, Jörgen," as if he'd told her a rude joke. There was something of an age gap between them. I estimated it to be at least ten years.

Beyond them sat John, a taciturn gentleman of about sixty, who worked on the financing of inspection visits, and next to him sat someone called Lisbeth, I think. I don't know. I wasn't about to ask. She hadn't introduced herself.

There were twenty-three of us in total and almost all had a screen or little wall of some sort around their desks. Only Håkan and I were stuck in the middle of the floor. Håkan said we would soon be getting screens as well, but I said it didn't matter.

"I've got nothing to hide," I said.

Eventually I found a rhythm in my fifty-five-minute periods, and a certain fluency in my work. I made an effort to stick to my schedule and not allow myself to be disturbed in the middle of a period with either coffee breaks, small talk, telephone calls, or trips to the toilet. Occasionally I felt like going for a pee after five minutes, but always made sure I sat out the whole period. It was good for the soul, character-building, and obviously the relief of finally easing the pressure was that much greater.

There were two ways to get to the toilets. One, round the corner past the green potted palm, was slightly shorter than the other, but because I felt like a change that day, I decided to take the longer route past the lift. That was when I stepped inside the room for the first time.

I realized my mistake and carried on past the large bin for recycled paper, to the door alongside, the first of the row of three toilets.

I got back to my desk just in time for the next fifty-five-minute period, and by the end of the day I had almost forgotten ever having looked through the door leading to that extra space.

4.

The second time I went into the room I was looking for photocopy paper. I was determined to manage on my own. Despite all the exhortations to ask about things, I was unwilling to expose myself to humiliation and derision by displaying gaps in my knowledge of the setup. I had come to recognize the little stress wrinkles they all got whenever I did actually ask. Obviously they weren't to know that I was aiming to get to the top of the Authority. To become someone who commanded respect. And I didn't want to give Håkan any excuse to indulge his work-avoidance.

So I checked everywhere, all the places where in the majority of offices you might expect to come across photocopy paper, but there was none to be found. Finally I made my way round the corner, past the toilets, where I had a feeling I had previously seen a small room.

At first I couldn't find the light switch. I felt along the walls on either side of the door, and in the end I gave up, walked out again, and found the switch on the outside. What an odd place to put it, I thought, and went back in.

It took a moment for the fluorescent light to flicker

into life, but I was quickly able to ascertain that there was no photocopy paper there. Even so, I got an immediate sense that there was something special about this place.

It was a fairly small room. A desk in the middle. A computer, files on a shelf. Pens and other office equipment. Nothing remarkable. But all of it in perfect order.

Neat and tidy.

Against one wall stood a large, shiny filing cabinet with a desk fan on top of it. A dark-green carpet covered the floor. Clean. Free from dust. Everything neatly lined up. It looked slightly studied. Prepared. As if the room were waiting for someone.

I went out, closed the door, and switched off the light. Out of curiosity I opened the door again. I got a feeling I had to check. How could I be sure the light wasn't still on in there? Suddenly I felt uncertain whether up or down meant on or off. The whole idea of having the switch on the outside felt strange. A bit like the light inside a fridge. I peered in at the room. It was dark.

5.

The next day my new boss came over to our desk in the big, open-plan office, with his thinning hair and cotton cardigan. His name was Karl, and the cotton cardigan wasn't very new, but looked expensive. He stopped next to Håkan and pointed out, without any introductory pleasantries, that my shoes were dirty.

"We try to think about the floor," he said, pointing at a metal basket full of blue plastic shoe covers hanging on the wall right next to the entrance.

"Of course," I said. "Naturally."

He patted me on the shoulder and walked away.

I thought it was strange that he didn't smile. Don't people usually try to smooth over that sort of remark with a little smile? To show that you're still friends, and make me, as the newcomer, feel welcome? It wasn't nice, getting told off as bluntly as that. It had a serious impact on my work and I sat there for a long while with an uncomfortable feeling that I'd just been taught a lesson. It was annoying that I hadn't thought about the shoe covers myself. Obviously I would have done it if I'd had time to think about it.

He had managed to make me feel both stupid and insecure, when in actual fact I was one of the smartest.

Besides, it was just rude to walk off like that. I counted the number of errors my boss had made during my short time there and came up with three. Plus one minor infraction. Three or four, then, depending on how you looked at it.

Håkan, who had obviously heard the whole thing, sat there unusually quietly, apparently preoccupied with some document. Carry on pretending, I thought. Carry on pretending.

I leaned down and undid my shoes even though I was in the middle of one of my fifty-five-minute work periods, and something like that really ought to be dealt with during one of the short breaks.

I looked around the room. Everyone was immersed in their own business. Yet it still felt as though they were all watching me as I walked, in just my socks, over to the small kitchen at the other end of the office and fetched a cloth. I cleaned up as best I could, fetched a pair of shoe covers, and put them over my shoes. They rustled as I took the cloth back. I tried to see if anyone else was wearing shoe covers, but they were all wearing either slippers or normal shoes. Maybe they were indoor shoes, I thought.

I wrote a note and stuck it on my briefcase:

Buy slippers.

Then I went to the coffee machine and got a cup of coffee. I reasoned that this fifty-five-minute period was already ruined. I would just have to sit it out and start again with the next one.

The bulb in the ceiling of the little kitchen was broken and needed changing. When I opened one of the cutlery drawers, I discovered that there were plenty of new bulbs there. It would be a painless task to unscrew the broken one and replace it with a new one. It seemed odd that no one had done anything about such a simple problem.

The coffee was far too hot to drink straightaway. I had to keep moving it from hand to hand to avoid burning my fingers, so I thought I might as well take a turn around the department and try to build up my social network.

First I went over and stood beside John's desk. But as I was standing there it struck me that it might be best to start with Ann, seeing as she, in purely geographic terms, was closest to me and Håkan. If I was going to expand my contacts, obviously I ought to start at the center and work my way outward. Like ripples in water, I thought. Besides, John made a hopelessly bland impression. What did someone like that have to offer me that I didn't already have? It would be unfortunate for my profile to be seen with such an insipid individual from the older generation, and thus become associated with the colorless crowd.

Ann was a woman, of course, and I was reluctant to associate too intimately with women and risk seeming pushy or ingratiating, but I realized I could adopt a gender-neutral attitude to start with. It ought to help my modern image and demonstrate a certain intellectual flexibility. Besides, Ann was looking more and more like the social queen of the department. Whether I liked it or not, she seemed to be something of a spider at the center of the web. I carried on to her desk and adopted a relaxed posture with my weight on one leg, so that she could be left in no doubt that I was amenable to having a conversation. She looked up at me and asked if I wanted help with something.

"No," I said.

She went on working.

I stood there for a while, looking at the badly drawn child's picture of a sunset, and wondered if she was aware of its flagrant inaccuracy. Maybe she was blinded by her emotional involvement? No matter what the circumstances, the child, or grandchild, deserved to be made aware of its mistake so that the error could be avoided next time. If things like that weren't pointed out, its marks for drawing would certainly be negatively impacted.

After a while I became aware that the zipper of my trousers, and thus my genitals within, were on exactly the same level as her face. So I shifted my body slightly to find a more neutral position and ended up standing right behind her chair, which also felt rather awkward. Particularly as she didn't seem remotely bothered by me. I blew gently on the coffee and waited for her to say something. It was starting to feel a bit uncomfortable just standing there. Jörgen looked up at me briefly and I decided to give Ann ten seconds. Once they had passed I walked away, taking with me the clear message: I wasn't welcome.

Håkan was sitting there typing, and I wondered if he was actually writing something or merely wanting to give the impression that he was busy.

He was wearing a shabby blue corduroy jacket, which made an unusually scruffy impression. Particularly when combined with his long sideburns, which somehow seemed better suited to the 1970s. I wondered why he hadn't taken it off. As I was sitting there looking at him, it struck me that his blue jacket had been bothering me since first thing that morning. Even before the business with the shoe covers and cloth, and before the incident with Ann, I seriously disliked that jacket. Once when he emptied his pockets out onto the desk I saw he had a whole bundle of crumpled napkins. Several of them appeared to have been used. He looked tired. Maybe he was out every night partying? Either way, he ought to take care to make sure that his work didn't suffer.

I never went into the room that day. But I thought about it several times. It was as if I was thinking: I ought to go into the room.

6.

That night I lay awake thinking about Karl's cotton cardigan and what sort of unfortunate consequences his attitude problem might have. I thought about Håkan and the way he got away with things. I thought about Ann and the elegant way she rejected me. I realized I would have to look out for her. She was doubtless capable of dragging a creative individual down to the semi-social state of casual interaction involving endless coffee and small talk that characterized most workplaces.

Oh well. I wouldn't let myself be affected.

Instead I thought about the attractive woman in reception. Her smile. The way she made me feel genuinely welcome each morning with just a glance. As if she really saw me. Saw that there was something special about me. I realized that she was one of the rare breed of alert women, of whom there are fewer and fewer, and decided as I lay there to give her a little of my time. Maybe a chat early one morning, maybe lunch?

In my mind, I went through material from the department. Decisions and framework documents that I arranged chronologically and put in folders. I got up, went out into the kitchen, and drank a glass of milk as I read the ads in the morning paper.

7.

The third time I went into the room, I did it for no reason. That's not like me at all. I usually stick to a clear chain of cause and effect, but this time it was as if I just wanted to go there. I closed the door and stopped in the middle of the floor, in front of the desk.

The desktop was partly covered by a protective pad that seemed almost to have been stuck down. I felt obliged to lift one corner to check that it was only held in place by the anti-slip backing that stopped it shifting even a millimeter in any direction, no matter how you pulled and pushed it.

In front of the pad was a hole puncher, a stapler, and a teak pen holder containing two ink pens and a pencil. All neatly lined up. All neatly lined up.

I raised my elbow and rested it on the shiny metal filing cabinet that stood against one wall. I felt a sense of calm in my body that seemed to cleanse my whole system. An intoxicating feeling of relaxation. A bit like a headache pill.

There was a full-length mirror in the room. I caught sight of myself in it and, to my surprise, I looked really good. My gray suit fit better than I thought, and there was something about the way the fabric hung that made me think that the body beneath it was—how can I put it?—virile.

I stood there for a long while, resting my weight on one leg, with my elbow on the filing cabinet. It was a good stance. I looked incredibly relaxed. Simultaneously confident and aware.

I had never thought of myself as "attractive." Most of the time I used mirrors to check that my clothes and accessories were in the right place. Not to check how "attractive" I was. The idea had never occurred to me. I never actually thought about men as being either more or less attractive. But I realized it was time to start doing so.

Because the best thing was the look in the eyes.

The man reflected in the mirror had a remarkable look of concentration in his eyes. He fixed me squarely with his pupils and followed me wherever I went. I realized at once that this was a new asset, a pair of eyes that could demand anything. And get it.

8.

Inhibited people don't see the world the way it really is. They only see what they themselves want to see. They don't see the nuances. The little differences.

A lot of people, more than you'd imagine, think everything's fine. They're happy with things the way they are. They don't see the faults because they're too lazy to allow themselves to have their everyday routines disturbed. They think that as long as they do their best, everything will work out okay.

You have to remind them. You have to show people like that what their shortcomings are.

Fresh documents kept arriving from the investigators. The numbers on the title page indicated the level of priority given to their conclusions, on a declining scale where number 1 was the most important. On the fourth floor we worked exclusively with three- and four-figure documents. The framework decisions from one to ten were almost never changed now, and those in double-figures were dealt with by considerably more senior administrators on the floors above. No one in my department had ever worked with a single- or double-digit decision. Not even Karl. As soon as anyone started working on a file near two or three hundred, rumors of promotion would start to circulate about the person in question. Fortunately for everyone on my floor, there were departments lower down that worked with all the five-figure material.

9.

The fourth time I went into the room I took my colleague Håkan with me. We had some questions about internal organization to go through, and I thought it best to discuss them inside the room.

Håkan sat on the other side of my desk. We worked opposite each other. At any moment we might happen to look up and meet each other's gaze. I tried never to look straight ahead whenever I looked up from my work. Håkan carried out his duties with the same lightness of touch as everyone else in the department. He used the phone more or less as he liked, took breaks whenever he felt like it. He would spend ages gazing off into the distance without it apparently having anything to do with work. Now and then he would try to talk to me as well. I would rebuff him gently but firmly. Usually with a simple gesture of the hand. Arm out, palm raised toward him. It worked.

We didn't actually share a desk. We each had one of our own. But the desks were positioned back to back and Håkan had an irritating habit of shoving his papers across his desk every time he started something new, which meant that they eventually ended up on my side.

One day I caught him in the process of doing precisely that. In the middle of one of my fifty-five-minute periods.

It certainly wasn't my intention to sit and stare at him as he worked, but his movements were so expansive that it was hard not to. He took out a couple of weighty new files from the investigators and put them in front of him on the desk, but instead of gathering up and tidying away what was already there, he merely pushed it away from him. Toward me.

I realized at once what was going to happen.

Not now, maybe not even today, but eventually Håkan's desktop would overflow with files and papers and documents, and they would begin to eat away at my side.

I had seen the same pattern before, in other workplaces, and knew it would be a source of irritation between us. I spent a little while wondering how best to tackle the situation on this occasion.

For the time being there was nothing I could say. He could manage or mismanage his desk however he liked as long as he kept to his side. There were still a few centimeters left as yet. Almost a decimeter. What could I say?

• • •

I looked at the time. There were still about twenty-five minutes left of my fifty-five-minute period, but my rhythm had been disturbed. I would just have to regard the rest of the period as lost.

At the same time, I realized that now that the thought of what was going to happen with Håkan's and my desks had arisen, it was going to be very hard to let go of. It would be there as a point of friction, and was bound to unsettle me. Maybe it would be just as well to deal with the confrontation at once, seeing as I now, in a manner of speaking, had some time to spare? At some point Håkan would have to learn to put things away before he started on something new. Not just push it away and assume that it would disappear by itself. Maybe it made sense to make him aware of that without delay?

I got up quickly. Walked behind my chair and stood there with my arms leaning on it. Took three deep breaths. Håkan looked at me and smiled a quick, false smile that was probably meant to look polite. I spun the chair gently, back and forth, as I looked at his papers.

I was very conscious of the fact that this was properly a matter for management. Efficiency savings of this sort and solutions to potential collegial conflicts naturally ought to be dealt with by an alert and engaged boss.

An attentive and empathetic leader would naturally have noticed the fissure that was on its way to breaking out within the ranks, and would have done something about it. Rather than waste time picking on the more alert members of staff about shoe covers.

But perhaps I recognized that Karl really did not possess those qualities? Perhaps I recognized even then that he wasn't management material, and that one day I instead would be taking control of this department? Perhaps this was the first step? Perhaps this was exactly the right opportunity for a rebuke?

"Håkan," I said in a friendly but firm voice.

"Yes," he said, looking up at me as if I were interrupting him in the middle of something important.

"Have you got a minute?"

He nodded.

I stretched, sucked in a deep breath through my nose, and let it out of my mouth in small puffs as I contemplated what tactics to employ.

"Look around you," I said eventually.

"Yes?" he said.

"What do you see?"

He said nothing for a short while as he looked around.

"No, I don't know . . ."

He went back to looking at his screen.

"I'd prefer us to deal with this at once," I said.

"With what? What do you mean?" he said, suddenly irritated.

I fixed my gaze on him and said in a calm and friendly voice:

"Before this gets out of hand, I'd like you to listen to me. I'm sure you'll see what I mean."

He looked at me with the tired, ignorant, slightly stupid expression that is so common in people who aren't used to seeing the broader picture in small things.

"Let's take a walk," I said, leading him round the lift and into the little room. I thought it best to deal with this in private, so that we could talk without being interrupted.

Inside the room the air was fresh and cool. I closed the door behind us and stood in front of the mirror with my arm on the filing cabinet. The light in the room definitely made Håkan look worse, while I glanced in the mirror and confirmed that I had retained the same crispness as last time. The man in the mirror was able to smile. He looked relaxed and spoke with a calm, deep voice.

"There's something I've noticed," I said.

"Yes?" Håkan said, looking round as if he'd never seen this room before. Perhaps he hadn't. He didn't seem to be particularly observant. Poor fellow. In just a couple of weeks my local knowledge had already surpassed his.

I decided to get straight to the point and if possible get back in time for the next fifty-five-minute period.

"You don't put your old files back when you take out new ones," I said.

"What did you say?" Håkan said.

"I said I've noticed that you're letting your papers spread out across your desk. Soon they'll be on my side, and then you'll be encroaching on my space. I am, as I'm sure you can appreciate, keen to have full access to the whole of my desk. I am already inconvenienced by the disproportionately large computer that takes up about a third of the space; it really ought to be possible to procure a system with more modern, smaller terminals, but never mind that, that isn't your responsibility. I would just like you to adopt new habits that don't risk disturbing my work. Do you understand?"

Håkan looked at me in surprise, as if he had been expecting something completely different. Perhaps he thought I had something private to say? Maybe he thought we had come in here to discuss personal matters? I felt a momentary satisfaction at having so quickly and concisely clarified the problem to him, presenting my demands without a lot of introductory small talk. Now the ball was in his court and he had little option but to accept my terms. After all, my wishes were in no way unreasonable. Sure enough, he made a slight nod.

"Good," I said. "Well, I suggest we get back to our duties, and if everything goes smoothly we need never mention this again."

I smiled at him, opened the door, and stepped out. Håkan followed me and we both went and sat down. He had a dried, white stain on his shirt, high up on one side of his chest. I noted that he sat and looked at me for a long while after we had returned to our places, without doing anything about his papers. I let him. Things need time to settle, I thought. Eventually the message would get through to him and hopefully lead to a more proactive way of dealing with his things. Presumably he wasn't used to being reprimanded in such a clear and effective way. You might as well get used to it, I thought. I might very well end up as your boss one day.

I leaned across the desk and whispered:

"Don't think of it as a reprimand. More as an observation."

"What?" he said, and I realized that he was playing along in our tacit understanding to let this stay between us. I nodded, leaned back, and mimed zipping my mouth shut, then locking it and throwing away the key.

10.

That night I went through my reprimand sentence by sentence, word for word, and it got better each time.

I put on a CD of Mozart's Piano Concerto No. 21, but soon swapped it for one of Sting's albums, only to switch to Dire Straits and then John Cougar Mellencamp. I didn't really feel like listening to any of them, but liked the idea of associating with the very best.

I went over to the windowsill in the living room and looked down at the courtyard. It was getting more and more like winter out there. The ground was already white and even more snowflakes were dancing in the light of the lampposts. I rolled my head a little to massage my neck, and counted the windows in the building opposite.

As I was about to go to bed I noticed my briefcase leaning against the wall. On the outside was a Post-it note. The glue had probably already left a mark on the leather.

11.

The fifth time I went into the room there was no reason at all. I had successfully completed my fifty-five-minute period of concentrated and undisturbed work, and felt no need of coffee or a trip to the toilet. I just went to the room because I liked it, and found a certain satisfaction in being in there.

Håkan hadn't yet found a better solution for his papers, which were still threatening to slip onto my side, even though a couple of days had passed since our conversation inside the room. Yet I still felt somehow calm about the matter. He probably didn't want to change his behavior just like that, after being ordered to do so. Possibly because he didn't want his colleagues to connect his sudden organized behavior with our meeting the other day, but possibly also to demonstrate a degree of independence toward me. That would pass. I couldn't deny him a degree of pride. If it turned out that he was consciously being obstructive and if things hadn't improved within a week, I would have to raise the matter again.

The open-plan office around me was full of protracted and completely unstructured discussion about the forthcoming Christmas party. It was about what games would be played, what sort of punch would be served, et cetera. Questions and ideas were tossed into the air and drifted around the office. The same individual subject was discussed in several places at once without there being any central focus, or even any contact with the actual party committee. I did my best to ignore the whole fractured debate, and naturally declined any involvement. When Hannah with the long ponytail, who seemed to have some sort of responsibility for the party, came over and asked if I wasn't going to consider attending, I used Ann's old trick of completely ignoring her and carrying on with my work. I actually thought about using her line, "Do you want help with something?," but when I turned round to deliver it Hannah had already gone.

12.

The sixth time I found myself in the room it was in the company of the woman from reception. Completely unplanned.

Late in the day I had decided to attend the Christmas party after all, because I realized that a certain amount of information of the more informal variety tended to flourish on such occasions.

"So you came in the end," Hannah with the ponytail said as I stepped out of the lift and saw that the entire office had been transformed.

There were sheets and various fabrics hanging everywhere. The lighting was subdued. It was hard to see. At first I considered not replying at all. Hannah with the ponytail was one of those women who laugh readily and can talk nonsense for hours without a single sensible thing being said. In principle I try to ignore people like that as much as possible. I simply choose not to think about them. Make up my mind that they don't exist. And I didn't think hers was a particularly pleasant way to greet guests. Especially not if you were one of the organizers. In the end I decided to give a clipped response.

"I did," I said.

"I mean, you didn't seem very keen," she said.

She stood there looking at me for a while in silence. I looked back, calmly and neutrally, until she spoke again.

"Well, we can probably find you a plate," she said, making it sound like a nuisance.

I realized a long time ago that dismissive remarks like that could easily be sexually motivated. Women of her age have that inverted way of approaching men of the same age. Particularly if you show a certain disinterest. I imagine it's to do with status and an unwillingness to show any sort of inferiority. A sort of liberation, maybe even feminism? My generation of women always have to show they're as strong as men, before finding clumsy ways of showing their affection.

I wasn't going to let myself be moved.

I got a glass of the tasteless, blue-colored punch that matched my blue shoe covers in a most irritating way. I realized once again that it was time to get a pair of those indoor shoes. But at the same time it didn't look like the other guests were paying much attention to the shoe code that evening. Some of them were definitely wearing the same shoes they had arrived in. I took a stroll past the glassed-off manager's office, trying to catch a glimpse of Karl's shoes in the crowd, but I couldn't see him anywhere.

He probably wasn't there, because the office had been rearranged in a way that it would be difficult for a boss to allow. The sheets had been fastened with a staple gun, which was bound to leave marks on the walls. Printers and phones and other electronic equipment had been covered in a way that was clearly a fire hazard. Who knows, maybe they had also blocked the fire escapes?

Here and there stood little clusters of candles, and someone had sprinkled some sort of glittery silver stars around them. A string of fairy lights had been hung from one wall to the other. It was supposed to be a Christmas decoration, but the whole thing had been done in a very amateurish way and didn't feel quite proper.

Somewhere a stereo was playing Christmas songs, but I never managed to identify where the noise was coming from.

People were standing in groups, noisily interrupting each other. It was obvious that they were all more relaxed than usual. Even John was participating in the small talk, which revolved around either the threat of cutbacks or the usual conversation about families and children and football.

I walked around among people who made various excruciating attempts to engage me in conversation. As you might imagine, it was a pointless task.

. . .

Outside the snow was still falling, and after a while I sank into one of the two leather armchairs over by the window, mainly to try out what it felt like. I'd just made up my mind to leave when the woman from reception came over and sat in the other chair. She looked very neat and clean. She had two glasses of wine in one hand and a napkin in the other. She smiled at me, the way she did every morning, and I asked why she was here, seeing as this wasn't her department.

"No, I know," she said, slightly embarrassed. "It's usually like this. I get invited to all the parties. I suppose everyone thinks I don't have a department of my own."

I did a quick calculation in my head.

"Let's see, there must be, what, eight departments?"

"Nine, actually," she said with a laugh. "The maintenance department invites me to theirs as well."

"That's not fair," I said, but she just laughed.

She took the napkin and started rubbing the bottom of her dress with it.

"Have you spilled something?" I asked.

"Well, I didn't," she said. "The punch splashed a bit, but I don't know. It's hopeless trying to get rid of stains like that. Especially if they've been there a while."

We sat in silence for a time as she rubbed her dress. Eventually she looked up at me.

"My name's Margareta, by the way."

"Oh," I said, then thought that I ought to say something more.

She looked as if she were expecting a reply, but what could I say? What could I possibly have to say about her name? Her name was Margareta. Okay. Good. Nice name.

I looked round the room. People were laughing and it was getting a bit loud. Every so often someone would shout something. The armchair was much less comfortable to sit in than I had imagined. I shifted my buttocks slightly to find a better position. On a small table between me and Margareta there was a large bowl of sweets. I looked at them, trying to work out if I wanted one.

"Don't think much of the fairy lights," I said after a while, pointing at the wall.

"No," Margareta laughed. "I think it was Jörgen who put them up."

"Oh," I said. "You seem to know a lot."

She laughed again. There was something about her laugh that, besides indicating a certain interest in me, also managed to put me in a good mood. It was clear that she was slightly intoxicated, which made her seem—

how can I put it?—more physical. It made me think of
Marilyn Monroe. But I didn't think that mattered much
at the time.

She raised one of the glasses and sipped the wine.

"Would you like a glass?" she asked, passing me the
other.

I shook my head and reached for the large bowl of
Christmas sweets instead. I fished out a toffee, which I
toyed with for a while.

I recalled a man from Denmark who took me on a
pub crawl once, and insisted on us drinking spirits all
evening. I felt sick for two whole days afterward.

"Come with me instead," I said, putting the toffee
in my pocket and pulling her gently but firmly with me
toward the little room beyond the toilets. Somehow it
felt like she appreciated the initiative, maybe even the
energy behind the decision and its implementation, by
which I mean the firm way of making a decision.

We slid round the corner behind the wall holding
Jörgen's fairy lights. I flicked the light switch outside
and she giggled like a little girl who was being allowed
to follow the naughty boy into his secret den.

13.

We entered the room just after half past ten in the evening, and I'd guess it was half past eleven by the time we emerged. What happened in between is in many ways still unclear.

Not that I was drunk. I still know what happened, but I'm not entirely sure how to interpret it.

We stood for a long time in front of the mirror. She touched me. I touched her back, but it was like she pulled my arms and hands to her, showing me round. Like a dance. I didn't have to move a muscle. She did it for me. Naturally, it was erotic, but never sordid the way it can so easily be when a man and woman meet. She smiled at me, but I can't remember us saying anything.

She had big, beautiful eyes and shiny hair. It was lovely. I was enchanted.

When we kissed it was as if she was me. I was me, but she was me too.

When we came out again she stood there looking at me for a long time. Charged. Changed. As if I'd shown her something entirely new. Something big. Something she hadn't quite been prepared for and didn't know how to handle. She turned on her heel and walked away. As far as I was aware, she went straight home.

As for me, I stayed for a while sucking the sweet.

14.

Someone had made a snowman in the courtyard below my window, but it wasn't very good at all. The two bottom balls were roughly the same size, and the top one was only marginally smaller, which meant that it didn't have anything like the traditional snowman shape that a snowman ought to have. And it didn't have a nose. Whoever had made the snowman hadn't bothered to find a carrot or anything else that would have functioned as a nose, and had just left it as it was. Maybe they had lost interest halfway through? Such is life, I thought.

That night I lay in bed and went through the evening, moment by moment. Over and over again. From the frosty greeting and Hannah's strange comments, to the encounter with Margareta from reception, to my strong sense of having been master of the situation. In some ways it was a novel experience. A feeling of power.

15.

Stupid people don't always know that they're stupid. They might be aware that something is wrong, they might notice that things don't usually turn out the way they imagined, but very few of them think it's because of them. That they're the root of their own problems, so to speak. And that sort of thing can be very difficult to explain.

I got an e-mail from Karl the other day. It was a group e-mail to the whole department. The introduction alone made me suspect trouble: "We will be putting staffing issues under a microscope."

Anyone with even a basic understanding of the language knows that you put things under "the" microscope, with the definite article. (Sadly this sort of sloppiness is becoming more and more common as text messages and e-mail are taking over.) I let it pass this time but knew that I would have to act if it happened again. I wondered what suitable comment about the proper use of language I could drop into the conversation next time I spoke to Karl.

16.

The morning after the party I got to work early.

A lot of the signs were still there. There was a sour smell, and plastic glasses and napkins on the floor. I wondered what preparations they had made for the clearing up.

"Things don't just clear themselves up, do they?" I said to Hannah with the ponytail when she arrived, still looking sleepy, a couple of minutes later. She glanced at me with annoyance, and I know she was impressed that I was there first, even though I wasn't part of any cleaning team. I sat down on the sofa by the kitchen and looked at a few newspapers, so that she would realize I had chosen to come on my own initiative rather than because I was told to.

After a while I noticed that she had chosen to start clearing up in a different part of the office, rendering my presence pointless. I folded the newspaper and went over to the lift.

I went down to reception and caught sight of Margareta hanging up her outdoor clothing in the little cloakroom behind the desk. I stopped beside the plastic Christmas tree and waited. From the other side of the counter I could see her standing in the little cloakroom adjusting her hair and clothes in a small mirror. Her skirt was nice, but she was wearing a dull-colored blouse that wasn't at all attractive. I'd have to remember to tell her not to wear it when she was with me if the two of us were going to get together, I thought. She must have felt she was being watched, because suddenly she started and turned toward me.

"Goodness, you startled me," she said.

"Did I?" I said. "I didn't mean to."

She gathered her things and came over to the counter.

"Early," she said, meaning me.

"Yes," I said, thinking that she seemed a little odd. She was being snappy in a way that I didn't appreciate at all.

I wondered whether I should say anything about the events in the room the previous day, but decided that it would be best to maintain a certain distance at first, and simply ride the wave of the impressions I had been given yesterday. I tried to remember what we had said to each other. What kind of agreement we had reached, so to speak. Eventually I said: "You too."

We stood there in silence for a while. She was arranging some papers on her side of the counter. Opening a large diary. Pulling a page off the calendar. People started to stream in. Margareta greeted almost all of them in an equally warm and friendly way, which put me in an even worse mood seeing as she really ought to realize that she was devaluing the impact of her smile if she used it on everyone. Didn't she know that she should hold back a bit?

I tried to look as though I had business down there. I started to leaf through a trade magazine that was on the counter, and after a while I went over to the coffee machine and pressed the button to get a cup. I stood there for a long while waiting for the coffee to start trickling down into the cup. I pressed the button a few extra times, and had managed to get fairly annoyed by the time I realized that I hadn't put any money in.

I couldn't help noting how much better the organization worked down here, where you had to pay for coffee, compared to the lax coffee-drinking that pertained up in my department where anyone, at any time, could scuttle off and get coffee without any restrictions at all.

When I was putting the coins in I realized that I was a couple of kronor short. I went back to Margareta and asked if she could lend me two one-krona coins. She was standing talking to a woman in a suit and didn't answer me at first, so I asked again. Slightly louder. Then she turned toward me with irritation and said that she could. She went into the little cloakroom and got her handbag, took out her purse, and passed me the coins. I thought it impractical to keep her handbag containing her purse so far from the counter, but said nothing. Partly because I didn't think her behavior deserved to be rewarded with my advice, and partly because I didn't want to appear too superior to her at such an early stage of our relationship. Instead, I merely smiled and decided to counter her irritation with a forgiving, worldly attitude.

"After all, two kronor isn't the end of the world," I said, glancing toward the woman in the suit, but there was no conspiratorial smile.

They resumed their conversation and I went back to the coffee machine, put my money in, got my coffee, then went and stood beside the plastic Christmas tree again. By now most people had arrived and the reception area resumed its usual deserted appearance. I was left alone again with Margareta on the other side of the counter.

"Well," I said after a while, sipping the hot coffee and wondering what I ought to say.

She looked up at me from her papers, but I saw none of the respect you might expect from a receptionist of her level. It made me slightly annoyed. Maybe she was one of those people who thought it was acceptable to set aside all politeness and manners once you've been introduced and become acquainted.

"Yes?" Margareta said.

I decided to sit her out. Let her catch up and realize

the situation she was in. Any moment now everything ought to click into place, I thought, but she just went on looking at me with that indirectly arrogant expression, rather like a mother looking at her teenage son.

When she didn't say anything, I felt obliged to speak: "Well, I thought it was nice, anyway."

She took a paper clip and fastened several documents together, then put them on a new pile.

"I have to ask you something personal," she said after a while, as she pushed the papers away. "Is that okay?" I nodded and she looked round. I could see she was gathering herself.

"Are you on drugs?"

At first I thought she was joking. I laughed, but then I saw that she was serious. I took a couple of steps back and noticed that I'd spilled some coffee on the sleeve of my jacket. What did she mean? Why would she ask that? Was she on drugs? Did she want me to join her on some sort of junkie adventure?

I must have looked angry because suddenly she got that scared look in her eye that I recognized from the night before. I wasn't used to people looking at me that way. It unsettled me, and made me even more angry.

"What do you mean?" I tried to say in my usual

voice, but I heard it come out much more strained than I had intended.

It annoyed me that she had so suddenly managed to throw me off balance. I wasn't remotely enjoying the confusion she was spreading, and felt the need to create more distance. I backed away another couple of steps.

"I just mean . . ." Margareta began uncertainly. "Well, what are you doing down here now, for instance? In work time?"

I looked at the large clock on the wall behind the desk and saw to my surprise that it was already twenty-five to ten. How could it be so late? So quickly?

17.

I left at once. Without a word I hurried across the granite floor and went up in the lift. I got off at the fourth floor and made an effort not to run to my desk. I slipped onto my chair and leafed quickly through my diary to check that I hadn't missed a meeting, but there was nothing written down. I glanced over at the glass doors where Karl sat, but couldn't see him. I took a deep breath and suddenly realized how tired I was. I tried to remember when I had last slept.

I should have seen through her earlier. Obviously she was a junkie. All that smiling. That optimistic outlook. It was a chemically produced friendliness. I'd walked straight into the trap. Being taken in by the surface appearance of a drug user was one of the dangers of being an open, honest person. Never suspecting anything.

I realized that I would have to stay away from her in the future.

I raised my head and tried to look straight ahead, but it was hard to get my gaze to settle on anything. I have to find somewhere I can pull myself together, I thought. I got up and felt my whole body aching with tiredness.

Without knowing how it had happened, I felt something warm and wet on my legs. I looked down and saw the remains of the coffee on my jacket and trousers, the empty plastic cup upside down in my hand. Slowly but surely I made my way toward the corridor with the toilets, then in to wipe the coffee off. I pulled out a bundle of paper towels and pressed them against my jacket and trousers.

The room, I thought. I'll go into the room for an hour. I crept out into the corridor, past the big recycling bin, switched on the light, and opened the door for the seventh time.

18.

I could feel the clean white wall against my back. The gentle texture against the palm of my hand as I placed it on the wallpaper. The cool steel against my cheek as I leaned my head on the filing cabinet. The soft motion of the drawers as they slid in and out on their metal runners. Order.

I counted the lengths of wallpaper on the long wall. Five, I made it.

After a short while I felt brighter. I looked at myself in the mirror and saw that I was my old self again. I looked better than I deserved to. I adjusted my tie and went back out into the office.

19.

I sat down in my place and looked at the time. I had about fifteen minutes left until a new fifty-five-minute period started, so I leaned back and stretched my arms up in the air. Then let them fall and folded them behind my head. I glanced over at Karl's glassed-in office. I didn't mind if he did see me now. See me taking time for myself. I sat for a while, going through various replies to things he might say. Little hints that would slowly but surely make him realize that I was a man of the future. Someone worth keeping in with. Not the sort of person to pick unnecessary arguments with. About trivial things.

I looked over toward the little kitchen with the broken light above the stove that still hadn't been fixed. It seemed astonishing that it was still like that. Was it really so hard to screw in a new bulb?

I sighed, tilted my head back, gazed up at the ceiling, and looked at the various fittings. The cables for the fluorescent lighting were attached to the outside of the ceiling tiles, fixed in place by little clamps that made the whole thing look rather provisional. A sausage-like cornice between the ceiling and the walls. I counted the lengths of wallpaper along the wall by the toilet corridor, and made it sixteen.

For some reason I thought that was rather low, so I counted them once more. And made it sixteen again. I spun gently in my chair and wondered how that could be right. Each length must be about half a meter wide, making eight meters for the whole wall. I looked down at the bookcases and filing cabinets lined up against it and tried to work out the distance. Yes, eight meters, that could be about right. But there were five lengths inside the room alone. How narrow could the toilets be, lined up alongside it? I wondered. They couldn't be less than one meter. Not when you took the walls into account.

I got up from my chair and went over to the wall. I stood there for a while looking at it. Three bookcases, a filing cabinet, and a photocopier were lined up against it. I went round the corner into the toilet corridor. There were the three toilets. The first one was vacant and I stood in the doorway and held my arms out to measure it. It must be at least a meter, I thought. I went back out into the corridor, past the room and the big green recycling bin, and reached the lift. I looked at it.

Then I went round the far corner and came to the wall with the bookcases and filing cabinets again. I backed away slightly and counted the lengths of wallpaper again. Sixteen.

I went up to the wall and put my lower arm against the wallpaper. I had heard somewhere that a grown man's lower arm and hand together make up about half a meter. That seemed to fit.

Once again I went back round the corner to the toilet corridor. Three toilets, a recycling bin, and a lift, all of which combined came to about eight meters. So what about the room?

I went back and sat down at my desk, took out a pad of graph paper, and did a simple sketch of this part of the fourth floor.

Impossible, I thought as I looked at the sketch. There's something that doesn't make sense.

I put the pad down and went round to the lift. I went down and got out on the third floor. It was almost as empty as the fourth floor. A man in a cap said hello to me as I went round the corner into their toilet corridor. I didn't bother to respond. I was taken by surprise, and because I didn't know him I didn't think there was any reason for us to waste time saying hello to each other. Besides, I was busy with this peculiar discovery, and I wasn't about to be sidetracked. I was on the trail of something. I could feel it in my whole body.

The layout was the same down here, toilets and recycling bin. But no room.

I went round to the other side where a large whiteboard had been screwed to the wall. I counted the lengths of wallpaper. Sixteen. Exactly the same proportions, I thought. It's all here. Except the room.

I took the lift back up again and stopped on the office side of the wall.

I looked at Jörgen's fairy lights up by the ceiling. They stretched all the way from one wall to the other, and down to the electric socket by the floor.

I grabbed hold of the string of lights, unplugged it from the wall, and pulled it down from the ceiling. It was more firmly attached than I had expected and when I finally managed to get the whole string loose, small flakes of plaster broke away from the top part of the wall.

I tied the part of the wire that had been hanging down toward the electric socket, then went round and laid it out on the floor on the other side where the toilets started. It reached just past the green recycling bin.

I knew it, I thought, then said it out loud to myself so that I would be sure to understand.

"It's invisible. It's a secret room."

I heard someone say my name. I turned round and caught sight of Ann in the doorway to one of the toilets.

Her face was completely blank. She was staring at me, so
I spoke as calmly as I could to her.

"Have you got a ruler?"

"What did you say?" she asked.

"A ruler?" I said. "Or a tape measure?"

She shook her head.

20.

I got the long ruler from Håkan's desk. It was fifty centimeters long. He'd borrowed plenty of things from me. It was only fair that I finally had a good reason to borrow something from him.

I started with the photocopier wall, in toward the office, and measured along the carpet. "8:40," I wrote on the sketch on my pad.

On the other side I sat down and started measuring the carpet where the first toilet started. I held my thumb in place, moved the ruler, and counted the number of lengths as I did the calculation in my head.

When I reached the lift I had got to 12:20. Impossible, I thought. That makes three meters and eighty centimeters that don't exist on the other side.

I went and stood by the lift to see if the corridor was angled somehow in a way that would distort the measurements, but the wall and corridor were perfectly parallel.

It was an excellent viewpoint. From there you could clearly see that the corridor ran parallel to the wall on the other side. No distortion, no angles. But with one room too many on one side. It was extremely professionally done.

21.

"Can I ask you something?" Håkan said when I gathered up my things at the end of the day. I had just decided to stop lending him my Staedtler pens with the 0.5 and 0.05 millimeter tips, seeing as I had noted that he seldom, if ever, put the lids back on them. Next time I would say no.

"Yes," I said. "Go ahead."

"What are you doing?" Håkan said.

I took my coat and scarf off the hanger and went round to Håkan. We were almost the only people left in the office. Lena by the window was still there, as she usually was.

"What do you mean?" I said.

Håkan folded his arms, leaned back in his chair, and looked at me.

"What are you doing when you stand like that?"

"Stand? Like what?"

"When you stand still like that. By the wall."

"Which wall?" I said.

He nodded his head toward the toilet corridor.

We both fell silent and looked at each other. I realized that this was a defining moment. A moment when

I might be able to find out what was really going on in this department.

"Come on," I said. "Show me. Where do I stand?"

Håkan squirmed and suddenly didn't seem so interested anymore.

"Oh, you know."

"No, show me. Where do I stand?"

He hesitated. He ran the fingers of one hand through his hair, down his cheek, and under his chin. He scratched his long sideburns. It was obvious that he felt unsettled.

"Look, never mind. We can talk about it some other time."

He slowly gathered together his things on the desk. I caught him glancing over toward Lena by the window.

"No, show me now," I said. "What do I do?"

"Come on, surely you know?"

"No. I don't know."

He folded his arms again and looked me in the eye.

"You stand there, completely still," he said.

"Where do I stand?"

"Over there. By the wall."

"Show me, Håkan. Please. I want you to show me exactly."

Håkan looked at me suspiciously. Finally he got up and went off round the corner. I followed him. We stopped right outside the door to the room.

"Here," Håkan said.

"What do I do here?" I said.

"You stand here. Completely still."

"Do I?"

"Yes, it's almost a bit creepy. You're so bloody still. How can you do that, without moving a muscle? It's like you're just not there."

"Show me."

"No."

"Go on, please."

"No, damn it. You just stand here completely still."

"Do I say anything?"

"No, you're completely gone. It's like you're somewhere else. Completely out of reach. Hell, your phone even started to ring in your inside pocket. I asked if you weren't going to answer it, but you didn't move a millimeter. It was like you couldn't hear. As if you were somewhere else."

"When did I do this?"

"The other day. You made me come with you. And then you just stood there like that."

"How long do I stand like that?"

"It varies. Last time it was about five minutes, but last week you must have stood for at least fifteen minutes."

"Has anyone else seen me like that?"

Håkan shuffled uncomfortably.

"Well, yes. People have to go to the toilets."

"So they've seen me."

"Yes, I mean, it's not like they stand and stare, but they can't help wondering. Me too. What is it you're doing?"

I looked him in the eye and he looked back. We looked at each other as if we were playing some sort of game where you had to make the other person laugh or look away. I thought it felt uncomfortable and somehow infantile. I felt a sudden burst of impatience. Was this the start of a message? Some sort of code that would initiate me into the secret? Was he trying to tell me something, or was this whole thing a test?

"Can I ask you something, then?" I said.

"Sure," Håkan said.

"What do you see in front of you here?" I said, pointing at the door.

22.

Håkan was wearing his rather worn, dark-blue corduroy jacket that day, and I could feel that it was having a negative effect on me. Blue really wasn't his color, and the corduroy was soft and threadbare. No substance to it at all. It made me think of poorly stuffed cushions in waiting rooms. It was making me uneasy and unfocused. And even more angry.

It was as if he wasn't properly concentrating on work.

There was something about him that had long made me suspect that he had a hidden agenda beyond the watchful eye of the Authority. His hair, his sideburns, and that scruffy jacket; it all suggested a set of values different from the ones that we in the department live by.

"Shall we go home now, Björn?" he said.

"Not before we're done here," I said.

As Håkan reluctantly explained, for the second time, what he could see in front of him, and stubbornly denied the existence of the room, I realized that I was going to have to be more obvious. I reached out my arm and pointed, so the tip of my forefinger was touching the door.

"Door," I said.

He looked at me again with that foolish smile and glazed expression.

"Wall," he said.

"Door," I said.

"Wall," he said.

23.

The following day I decided to pay careful attention to everyone going down the corridor, and I was forced to admire the elegant artistry of whoever had constructed the secret space. What had the architect done to conceal a room so effectively, when it was right in front of the noses of everyone working here? And who had managed to get them to act so credibly as if it didn't exist? Who had drilled this crazy exercise into them? And what was that room, really? Maybe it was dangerous, or did it possibly contain classified information? It seemed so unassuming, but perhaps that was the whole point? Maybe it was supposed to look innocent.

Just before lunch I went over to Jörgen. I stood there waiting until he looked up from his papers.

"Did you want something?" he asked.

I beckoned him toward me with my forefinger but he didn't move from his chair. His jaw was hanging like a boxer's.

"Have you got a minute?" I asked when he didn't obey my signal, which couldn't possibly have been unclear.

Finally he got the message and slowly followed me round the corner into the corridor. I stopped outside the door to the room, just as I had done with Håkan the day before. I made an effort to adopt a confidential tone of voice.

"Jörgen," I said. "I want you to be completely honest now. I want you to tell me what this room is for."

"What room?"

"This one," I said, touching the door with my finger.

"There's the lift," Jörgen said. "And there are the toilets."

"Mmh, but what about in between them?"

"In between? Well, there's a recycling bin, if that's what you mean . . ."

"That's not what I mean," I said. "What's this room for?"

I slapped my hand on the door, fairly hard. Actually harder than I had expected. I realized that this nonsense was wearing my patience. I had to try to keep a cool head.

"Well . . ." Jörgen said, looking at me.

I could see that he was extremely uncertain. He was evidently disconcerted at having to talk to me.

". . . it's a wall."

I glared at him.

"Is that all you've got to say?"

"Yes, what do you want me to say? You're fucking weird, you know that? Why are you so interested in this wall? Don't drag me into this."

I realized that Jörgen wasn't the right place to start. He was only a poor subordinate. Loyal, but entirely without influence. Whoever was responsible for this deception was on a different level of the hierarchy. I patted him on the shoulder and said he could go back in and sit down again.

That afternoon I went round and led my other colleagues to the same spot and carried out the same procedure as with Jörgen and Håkan. They were all reluctant, and they all stuck to the same story: there was no door there, let alone a room, and, anyway, what was I doing when I stood there without moving?

A certain anxiety spread through the department. People stood and whispered to each other. Håkan tried to put his arm round my shoulders and a number of people pointed at me. In the end I lost patience and gathered all the staff together, apart from Karl, who was off at some meeting all day.

I went from desk to desk and summoned everyone in friendly but firm terms to a short meeting. Some of them muttered, wondering what this was all about, wanting to know in advance. Some of them literally required a helping hand to get moving. But most of them came along without any fuss, and I told them all it would be best, as well as easiest, if everyone was given the information at the same time. Jörgen and Håkan laughed rather nervously at first and tried to make a joke of it, but when they realized that no one else thought they were very funny they quieted down noticeably. I herded them like a sheepdog out to the corridor, past the toilets, toward the room.

When I stepped inside the room for the eighth time, I had the whole department with me, apart from Karl. Each and every one of them stepped through the door, and once I had them all in there I explained to them that I had seen through their little joke. I said I didn't know who was the brains behind it, but that I'd worked it out well enough to let them know.

24.

That night I lay in bed, still feeling the congenial inner calm that only arises when you've discovered, grappled with, and successfully resolved a problem. I read four pages in the last but one issue of *Research and Progress*, and listened to Madonna's "Ray of Light" on the radio before I turned out the bedside lamp and fell asleep.

25.

The next day the whole department was called to Karl's office. It was quite a squeeze, but Karl said it would work if we squashed up a bit. Håkan was wearing a black jacket and I felt at once that I was much happier with it. It had a decent, classic cut and looked relatively new. It made him fit in better with the rest of us, and made me feel calm.

Everyone was talking at the same time. Once the whole team had gathered Karl knocked on his desk.

"Okay, everyone. Right, Ann, there was something you wanted to discuss?"

"Yes," Ann said, blushing. "Not just me. I think I can speak for the whole department . . ."

She fell silent, as if she were waiting for some show of agreement from the others.

"Well?" Karl said, looking around at the others. It was clear that he found this situation uncomfortable. Never previously had we all had cause to gather inside his office. Something was obviously going on. He turned toward Ann again.

"Maybe you'd like to start, then?"

Ann cleared her throat, and it looked like she was

standing on tiptoe as she talked. It made her look a bit like a schoolgirl. Even though she was over fifty.

"I . . . we think this business is all getting a bit unpleasant, Björn," she said, looking at me.

Everyone turned toward me.

"What's unpleasant?" I said.

"Shall we let Ann finish without interrupting?" Karl said, completely unnecessarily, because obviously I was going to let her finish. But all of a sudden it was as if his supposition that I had interrupted her were true. I could feel everyone's attention focus on me even more intently.

"Yes," Ann went on. "We're all getting worried. About you."

"Why would you be getting worried?"

"Well, when you stand there like that."

The room was silent for a long while. It was as if everyone had suddenly realized how absurd the situation was. They were looking at me, and I realized that I was supposed to say something. I stood there without speaking for a few more seconds, trying to look as many of them as possible in the eye. Then I lowered my gaze and sighed.

"Didn't we deal with this yesterday?" I said, raising

my head and looking from face to face. No one said anything.

"Didn't I tell you it was pointless trying to conduct
psychological warfare against me? I don't fall for that
sort of thing. No matter how well you synchronize your
stories."

Karl cleared his throat.

"What are you talking about, Björn?"

"I'm talking about systematic bullying," I said in a
fairly loud voice, so everyone could hear, while I pushed
my way through toward Karl's desk.

"Bullying that has evidently been going on for several weeks."

I twisted round so that the others could see me properly. I touched the collar of my jacket so that a little of
the lining became visible. I thought it made a good impression.

"To start with, I've noticed that some people in here
have adopted an unnecessarily harsh tone, and have
demonstrated a rather unpleasant attitude toward me
and not made any great effort to make me feel welcome.
This is probably because you're unsettled by me. There's
nothing strange about that, creative people have always
encountered resistance. It's perfectly natural for more
straightforward individuals to feel alarmed by someone

of talent. I would imagine that this has its origins in the fact that one or more of you have observed that I have taken the liberty on two or three occasions to take myself aside and gather my strength alone, having a short rest in that little room beside the lift. To some extent I can understand that this might strike some people as annoying. Obviously, we need to do our work and not take breaks whenever we feel like it, but I can assure you all that I have always taken care to make up for any concomitant loss of efficiency. And if it is the case that you have any secrets in there which for some reason you don't want me to see, you're welcome to tell me. Right here."

"As I understand it," Karl began, but now it was my turn to speak.

"You haven't understood anything," I said. "On the contrary, you've kept your distance. And in the meantime one or more individuals have taken it upon themselves to play some sort of psychological trick on me. Instead of coming straight out and having a normal discussion, a decision has been made to test my limits."

"Who—?" Karl began.

"Everyone," I interrupted. "Who knows, maybe you yourself are involved somehow?"

"I don't think so," Karl tried once more.

"Would you mind waiting with your analysis until all the facts are on the table?" I said, in a reasonably stern voice.

Karl fell silent again. It was obvious that he had nothing to offer in response. He stood there stiffly and listened as I went on.

"I have reason to believe that my—shall I say closest?—colleague, Håkan here . . ."

I pointed at Håkan, who immediately looked down and began to scratch his sideburns.

". . . is one of the people behind this. At least he was the first person to raise it with me."

I let the accusation sink in, then turned back to face Karl again. I fixed him with a steady gaze.

"I have no great expectation that you will be able to resolve this situation, Karl. But I presume you can't bury your head in the sand indefinitely, and that that's why you've called this meeting. It can't be any secret that you feel threatened by me, and would like to get rid of me, which is why I'm taking the liberty of uncovering this charade. This attempt to destroy me."

There was absolute silence in Karl's office. Everyone was standing completely still. The only thing disturbing the silence was the rustling from my blue shoe covers as I turned to inspect the stunned workforce.

"Try to see this as a learning experience," I went on

in a somewhat gentler tone. "If we all go back to our respective duties and never mention this incident again, embarrassing as it is for everyone—if everyone can promise to be open and honest from now on, and never try to play similar tricks on me to unsettle me, then I am prepared to forget the whole business. Simply because I am all too aware that intelligence and talent always upset people of more average abilities. For that reason alone, I am prepared to forgive you. Little people can't always be held accountable for the fact that they sometimes feel drawn to ruin and undermine their betters."

There was total silence for something like twenty seconds. It was as if no one in the room had properly understood what had happened. I looked at Karl, who just stared back. This time he had met his match. After a while I realized that I was going to have to take charge.

"You can go now," I said.

One by one they went back to their desks. A breathless procession of subdued employees dispersed around the department.

26.

Karl ran his hand over his thinning hair. He had tiny beads of sweat on his brow. Almost imperceptible. He craned his neck and loosened his tie slightly. I sat down on the comfy armchair opposite him, although it was a bit lower than the office chair he was sitting on. Karl slumped down in his chair. He sat there in silence for a long time, massaging his temples with two fingers on each side. Eventually he sighed.

"How are you feeling, Björn?"

"Fine, thanks," I said.

He rolled his chair closer to his desk, leaned his elbows on it, and rested his chin on his clasped hands.

"You appreciate that you simply can't behave like this?"

"How so?"

"This sort of performance. It's unacceptable."

And then once more, as if he thought I hadn't heard him, or simply needed to repeat it to himself:

"Unacceptable."

"The way I see it," I said, crossing one leg over the other, "they simply need a strong hand. This sort of collective bullying only arises when people feel lost and—"

"Björn, Björn."

Karl raised one hand in the air. He leaned toward me.

"I'm in charge here. You do know that, don't you?"

"Yes," I replied.

I nodded.

"Don't worry about personnel matters, Björn. I can deal with those."

He leaned back in his chair again. Rubbed his chin with his hand and looked at me.

"Björn," he said. "You pulled down the Christmas decorations and damaged both the wall and ceiling."

I nodded.

"That was careless of me."

"And the fairy lights themselves . . . well, they're evidently broken now."

"I shall reimburse you for the damage," I said. "How much?"

"Well, the wall and ceiling will be all right. It's probably time for them to be redecorated anyway. But the Christmas lights were Jörgen's personal property."

We sat and looked at each other for a long while without speaking. Finally he leaned forward.

"This . . . room . . ." he began.

"I'm glad you raised that," I said.

He looked out at the open-plan office.

"Where do you say . . . ?"

"Right next to the lift, to the left of the recycling bin, next to the toilets."

"In the corridor?"

"Correct."

He sat in silence for a long time, and after a while I began to wonder if he had started to think about something else. In the end he spoke again.

"What sort of room is it?"

"As far I can tell, it's not being used, and hasn't been for some time. I haven't made a mess or touched anything. If anything shady is going on in there, I don't know anything about it. I've just gone there when . . ."

I paused for a moment, trying to find the right words, the correct way to describe what I did there. "To recuperate" sounded feeble somehow, and besides, it was more like I was "recharging my batteries." I tried a different tack.

"The strange thing is that I've made some calculations. I've measured the surrounding area, and I can't quite make it fit . . ."

I wondered how much of this I ought to reveal to him. It was beyond question that I was the subject of a comprehensive and well-thought-out prank, and I didn't want to appear stupid. I tried laughing about it.

"Ha, this trick with the walls . . . I really can't work

out how they've done it. In purely architectural terms. Well, it's certainly been very cleverly done . . . Very cleverly done."

He looked at me, a whole series of lines on his forehead.

"What do you do there?" Karl asked.

"In the room?" I said.

He nodded.

"After first carrying out a visual check, I usually just . . . spend time there."

"But," Karl said, "what exactly do you do?"

"Nothing," I said. "But I can appreciate if it upsets—"

Karl interrupted me again.

"Never mind about the others now, Björn. Why do you want to spend time there?"

"I. Well—how can I put it?—I take energy from it."

He sat in silence for a while, just looking at me.

"Okay," he suddenly said, leaning forward. "Are you finding it difficult, working here for us?"

I looked at his perspiring temples and wondered who was finding it more difficult. Then I leaned back and said:

"Not particularly."

"Is there anything you'd like to talk to me about?"

I wondered if I ought to raise the subject of correct linguistic usage, but somehow this didn't feel like the right moment. I decided to give a more sweeping answer that would be bound to arouse his curiosity and throw a wrench in the works:

"There's plenty to talk about with this department."

"I see," Karl said. "Such as what?"

"Well. I don't want to mention anyone by name. But I can say that more than one person here at the Authority is a drug user."

"Drugs?"

"Oh, you didn't know?"

He sat for a moment just looking at me.

"Does that have anything to do with this room?"

"Not in the slightest," I said.

"Mmm," Karl muttered, then sighed again.

He stood up and went over to the window, and stood there with his back to me for a while. Drumming his fingers lightly on the glass. He turned round, sat back down, and looked me in the eye. It was as if he was building himself up.

"There is no room, Björn."

"Yes there is," I said.

"No," he said.

"Yes, just behind—"

"Listen to me carefully now, Björn. There is no room next to the lift. There has never been a room there. It's possible that you've convinced yourself that there is. Maybe it's there for you, I don't know how that sort of thing works."

I raised a finger in the air and got him to shut up temporarily.

"If you're going to start——" I began, but he interrupted me immediately.

"That's enough!"

He stood up and came over to where I was sitting.

"Listen to me now, Björn," he said, in a surprisingly stern voice. "Whether or not there is a room there, I must ask you to stop going to it."

He waited for a second or two, just looking at me. I realized that for the moment it would be best to keep quiet, but I could feel my whole body wanting to move. The situation was reminiscent of when you've spent a long time sitting in a seat on a plane and just want to stretch your legs. He carried on in a considerably calmer voice.

"You have to appreciate that it upsets the rest of the group when they see you standing like that, in your own little world. It's perfectly all right if you want to do it at home. But not at work. You're scaring the staff. Don't you think you should try socializing with your colleagues a bit more? They say you hardly ever take a break."

"I have my own routine," I said.

"But it can be good to take a break every now and then."

"That's when I go into the room."

"But you can't go into the room anymore. Okay?"

I looked out through the window, with its surprisingly dull view of a deserted inner courtyard. It was the same snowstorm that had been going on for I don't know how long. The sun hadn't shown its face for several weeks. I met his tired gaze.

"What you're telling me now . . ." I began, but suddenly felt my voice fail me.

I lost my flow and could hear that I sounded as if I were about to start crying. I cleared my throat and once again shifted position in the chair.

"You have to understand," I said. "The fact that you're saying there is no room is just as strange to me as if I were to say that that chair isn't there."

I pointed at his office chair.

"This chair is here," he said.

"Good," I said. "At least we agree about that."

He laughed lightly and put his hand on my shoulder.

"Since the time we agreed to have you working here, things have evidently changed dramatically. I still thought you might be able to cope with the relatively simple tasks you were given. Sorting, archiving, et cetera. We knew you were a complex character, but no one mentioned anything about you being delusional."

He fell silent for a moment and looked out at the courtyard as well. Just like me.

"You'll just have to stop going to that 'room.' Otherwise we'll have to come up with a different solution for you. Do you understand me?"

He pointed at my feet.

"And can't you get hold of a pair of indoor shoes? With those silly plastic things it's like you're just asking to be bullied."

I nodded slowly and looked through the glass at the people working out there. None of them seemed interested in our conversation. Not a glance from any of them. But they must all be aware of what was going on in here. Had they done all their talking about this, about me, already? What else had they agreed on? Karl sighed and went on.

"And I must also ask you to agree to see a psychiatrist."

27.

The clinic had turquoise curtains, and all the weekly magazines were aimed at a female clientele. I pointed this out to a nurse, who just giggled and hurried on.

The little sofas in the waiting room were full of people with colds, and even though there was a space right on the end I chose to stand slightly off to one side. I rested my eyes on a pleasant picture of flowers and grasses by Lena Linderholm.

Twenty minutes after the allotted time a different nurse came out and called my name. She went with me down the corridor, knocked on a half-open door, showed me in, and then disappeared.

I stepped into a sort of treatment room containing a brown vinyl padded couch with a big roll of paper at one end. In the middle of the floor was a little cart with a stethoscope and instruments for measuring blood pressure. There was a muddle of probes and test tubes.

I couldn't see a chaise longue anywhere.

Sitting behind a computer was a fairly young man with one of those goatee beards that were popular for a while. He was wearing a pale-blue short-sleeved tunic with a name tag. "Dr. Jan Hansson," it said. He tapped on the keyboard and read something without taking any notice of me.

I waited politely for a good while, wondering if he was older or younger than me. I cleared my throat a couple of times, and was on the verge of turning and walking out when he finally looked up.

"Well," he said. Nothing more.

He clicked his mouse, got up from the chair, and came over to me. We shook hands. His hand was wet and smelled of rubbing alcohol.

"Jan," he said.

"Thanks, I noticed," I said, pointing at the name tag.

He gestured toward a chair next to a sink. On either side of the basin were two pressure pumps with containers attached.

"Please, have a seat," he said, sitting down on his own ergonomic office chair.

"Thanks, I'm happy to stand," I said.

He looked at me.

"Mmh, I'd prefer it if you sat down."

I sighed and put my coat over the back of the chair. I sat down reluctantly, perching on the edge of the considerably more basic chair.

"Okay . . . er . . ."

He rolled over to the computer and looked at the screen.

"Björn," he said. "What can we do for you?"

"I thought I was going to see a psychiatrist," I said.

"We'll start with me," he said. "Well?"

"I'd rather not say anything. I'd like you to make your own evaluation without any preconceptions."

He glanced at a large clock on the wall.

"It's going to be very hard for me to help you if you don't say anything, Björn."

"I'd like you to make your own evaluation."

"I don't know you."

"But you are a doctor?"

He nodded.

I thought for a moment, and then described objectively and in detail recent events in the office. About the room, and Karl, and the other staff. About ignorance, invisibility, and the withholding of information. The doctor listened, but I noticed one of his legs starting to twitch after a couple of minutes. He interrupted me in the middle of a sentence.

"I don't understand what sort of medical——"

"If you'll let me finish, it might be clearer then," I said.

He looked at me as if he were sizing up an opponent. And it amused me that for the first time since I entered the room he seemed a little dispirited. He was presumably used to harmless patients with no will of their own who just wanted medication, but here was something different for him. Someone made of sterner stuff. He leaned back, folded his arms, and listened with a forced smile on his lips.

When I had finished, he sat for a fair while just looking at me. On the wall behind him was an ugly picture of an apple, and another of a pear that was almost as bad.

"This room," he said. "What sort of room is it?"

"A normal room," I said.

"What does it look like?"

"It's an office."

"Where is it?"

"At work."

"I mean, where at work?"

I thought for a while about whether it would be okay to tell him about the ingenious architectural solution, because he must have some sort of duty of confidentiality, but I decided not to trust the goatee beard entirely and instead chose a middle way.

"It's between the toilets and the lift," I said.

"And you go in there?" he said.

"Yes, but they say I mustn't."

"Mmh," he said, feeling for a pen in his top pocket.

"What do you do there?" he said.

"I rest."

"You rest?"

"Yes."

He got the pen out and clicked it, making the point pop in and out. Back and forth.

"And you want to go on sick leave?"

"No."

"Oh. So what do you want?"

"I don't want anything. The company sent me here."

"Don't you work for an Authority?"

"I prefer to see it as a company. It makes my abilities sharper."

"Really?"

"Yes."

He looked at the computer and I wondered if he was really looking at anything or just trying to buy himself some time. I decided to try to answer his questions quickly, in order to throw the ball back into his court as soon as possible, so to speak. Clearly he was clutching at straws. Presumably he lacked the skill demanded for matters of this sort.

"Have you mentioned this to your colleagues?"

"My boss was the one who made me come here."

"Why?"

"He said I had to see you."

"Me?"

"Someone. He said I had to come here."

He nodded and spoke slowly, as if he were trying to slow the tempo. But I wasn't about to let myself be sunk.

"So that you could go on sick leave?"

"I don't want to go on sick leave."

"Because you went into that room?"

"Exactly."

"Why?"

"He says it doesn't exist."

"What?"

"The room."

"Your boss says the room doesn't exist?"

I was very pleased that I managed to say "yes" before he'd even finished his sentence, which I felt reinforced the impression that I was one step ahead of him. He nodded slowly.

"So does it?" he said after a pause.

"It does to me."

"Does it for anyone else?"

"They pretend it doesn't."

"Has anyone else been inside the room?"

"I don't know. They don't seem keen to go in."

"Why don't they want to go in?"

"I don't know. They say it doesn't exist."

"But you know that it exists."

"It exists."

"And it's an office?"

"Yes."

"A perfectly ordinary office?"

"Yes."

He fell silent for a while, clicking his pen.

"Is there anything else in there?"

"Anything else?"

"Yes. Are there things in there?"

"Of course there are things."

"What sort of things?"

"Do you want me to . . . ?"

"Yes, please."

"Well, there's a desk . . ."

"Yes?"

"And a lamp. Computer, folders, a filing cabinet, and so on."

"Yes?"

"Pens, paper, a hole puncher, a stapler, Wite-Out, tape, cables, a calculator, a desk mat, all sorts of things."

"Yes?"

"Yes."

A nurse knocked on the door.

"Are you nearly done?" she whispered.

I wondered what it was we were supposed to be done with, but the doctor just nodded at her, looked at the large clock on the wall, and went on.

"Have you ever had any psychiatric treatment in the past?"

"Of course not," I said.

"Any counseling when you were in your teens?"

"Hardly."

"You're not on any medication?"

I shook my head.

"What about alcohol?"

"What do you think?"

"I'm asking you. Drugs?"

"No more than you," I said.

He shut his eyes and blew the air out of his mouth. He rubbed his eyes with one hand, and I carried on looking at him so that I could look him in the eye as soon as he decided to open them again.

"Do you feel unwell in any way?" he went on, still rubbing his eyes.

"Do you?" I said.

He shook his head and sighed.

"I honestly don't know what to do with you," he said after a brief pause.

"That doesn't surprise me," I said.

"You don't have to be unpleasant," he said.

"Nor do you," I said, as quickly as I could.

We looked at each other for a while. I was fairly pleased with the way this was going. I could tell he felt a degree of respect for me. You could see in his eyes that he wasn't used to getting this sort of response.

"Why are you here?" he said.

"Because I was sent here."

"Okay, you know what? I think you should contact us again if you feel worse. It's difficult for me to do anything about any other problems you may have at work."

He got up and went back to the computer.

"I was told I'd be seeing a psychiatrist," I said.

He shook his head gently.

"I don't know what grounds I could refer you on . . ."

"No, of course not," I said as I stood up and took my flattened coat from the back of the chair. "Maybe you could talk to someone who does know?"

"Do you know what I think?" he said, in a completely different voice, almost a whisper.

"No," I said, suddenly noticing the loud ticking sound that the big clock on the wall was making.

"If you'd like my own personal opinion," he said, "I'd have to say . . ."

"Yes, what would you say?"

He looked at me for a brief moment.

"I'd say that you're putting it on."

28.

Inside the room there was a calm. A concentration that felt like early mornings at school. It contained the same relaxed feeling and limited freedom. Each line seemed perfectly connected to the next. Everything messy and unsettling vanished. Precision returned.

I ran my finger over the desktop and felt the utterly straight line that was held at precisely the same plane by first the flawlessly sanded and varnished veneer chipboard, which in turn rested upon the perfect frame: spray-painted legs made of metal tubing. I was sure that a level would prove the evenness of this generously proportioned work surface.

Beneath the desktop, inside the legs on one side, was a varnished drawer unit on wheels with a cedar-wood frame. It was fronted by a matte wooden shutter that folded smoothly back along its rails as I put my palm on the front and slowly moved it upward.

The whole room breathed tradition. There was an air of old-fashioned quality to it. Is this what monks feel like as they walk the corridors of their monasteries?

On the desk was a low-energy lamp, 20 watts, attached to a clock of shiny, stainless steel. The armature of the lamp was adjustable. One setting for the strength of light. A firm base on the desktop.

By the side of the desk I discovered a lever that could be loosened so you could adjust the exact angle of the desktop. You could tilt the whole top to get the exact angle that you preferred. I adjusted it slightly to suit me, tilting it fractionally forward, downward, and felt how my other arm, which I had left idle, ended up in a perfectly relaxed position in which each part of the arm was firmly supported. Perfectly in tune with the furniture.

As I was sitting there my cell phone rang. I picked it up and answered it, and the sweetest music streamed out of it into my ears.

29.

The next morning we were summoned to another meeting in Karl's cramped office.

Karl tried to say something funny about small spaces, concluding with "tight passageways." No one laughed. I took this as further evidence of his incompetence as a manager. Naturally, he ought to have chosen a more neutral topic for humor, as there are plenty of innocent jokes about animals or ketchup bottles that didn't necessarily have any association to the conflict in which we found ourselves, and which could function more generally as a means of raising morale. If he felt he had to make a joke. Because this really wasn't amusing.

Håkan had sat down on the desk with Ann beside him. He was wearing his black jacket, and I definitely preferred it to the corduroy one, but I tried not to look at them. Jörgen and John were squashed up against the wall, and I couldn't help noticing that Jörgen kept nudging one of the big pictures, knocking it askew.

"I think this is very unfortunate," Ann said before Karl had even started. "Is he really going to stay? I mean, we said—"

Karl stopped her. He went behind his desk, and spoke in a loud, clear voice.

"Björn and I have had a little talk. Björn has been to see a psychiatrist. Together we have agreed to get rid of . . ."

He held his fingers up in the air on either side of his head to indicate quotation marks.

". . . 'the room' for the time being. Björn has promised . . ."

He turned to me.

". . . not to go there anymore. Isn't that right, Björn?"

I assumed I didn't need to nod. After all, everyone understood that I was party to this anyway. But Karl insisted.

"Isn't that right, Björn?"

I nodded. Karl went on.

"I think it's very useful for us to realize that we aren't all the same, and that some people see things in a—how can I put it?—slightly different way. But we're all adults, and we should be able to get along regardless. Shouldn't we?"

He looked around, but found no sign of agreement. In the end he turned to me.

"To emphasize the fact that this is a fresh start for you, Björn, I've taken the liberty of purchasing, at the expense of the Authority . . ."

He took out a bag containing a box and put it on the desk. He pulled out the box, opened the lid, and held up a pair of imitation leather indoor shoes.

". . . a small gift."

He handed them to me. I accepted them reluctantly.

"There you go," he said. "Now, I hope we can concentrate on our work from now on."

There followed five seconds of total silence. Then everyone started to talk at once.

"You mean he's going to stay?"

"Can't you see he's not right in the head?"

"What the hell is he doing here?"

"It's a health and safety issue."

"If he's allowed to carry on like that, I should be allowed to—"

"He's getting favorable treatment—"

"But he's mad."

"Really we ought to feel sorry for him."

Hasse from accounts shook his head slowly.

"Now that things are so tough here at the Authority, with the threat of closure hanging over our heads constantly . . . I mean, we really need to be functioning at full capacity. We haven't got time to be running some sort of day care center, have we?"

He looked round at the others. A number of them nodded. People starting talking all at once again. Karl managed to calm the mood temporarily, and Hannah with the ponytail tilted her head to one side as the prelude to a long-winded comment.

"It seems to me that management's way of dealing with problems of this nature indicates a certain degree of weakness."

Karl pinched the bridge of his nose with his fingers. Everyone seemed to be getting involved in the discussion, but none of them looked directly at me.

"He's a nutter, you have to admit that!" said a young man whose name I thought was Robert. He was about twenty and quiet as a mouse normally. I'd never heard him say a word before this. But evidently he felt he had to speak up now.

"According to the medical—" Karl began.

"But he's mad!" Jörgen said. "Anyone can see that. Surely we can't have a moron who goes and stares at the wall the minute things get busy?"

A few people laughed, which only served to spur Jörgen on.

"I mean, he needs treatment for that."

Hannah with the ponytail raised her voice.

"Although I do think we should all be allowed to do what we like during our breaks."

"I'm not so sure," Jörgen said, to even more laughter. "I say: fire him."

It was as if they all felt like laughing and were

prepared to grab any opportunity. Even though it really wasn't funny. Karl waved him off.

"We can't dismiss someone simply because they are——"

"But we're talking about someone who's mentally ill," Jörgen said.

"I'd like to point out," Karl went on, "that Björn has been carrying out his duties faultlessly."

Hasse spoke up again.

"Obviously he can do whatever he likes, but he keeps dragging the rest of us over there as well."

"Exactly!" Robert exclaimed. "Like that time he wanted the whole lot of us to go and stand there."

He looked round at the others, who nodded. Ann turned to address Karl with the whole of her feminine authority.

"I think it's creepy, seeing him stand there like that. He's so . . . It's like he's just not there."

As usual, several people decided to voice their agreement, and once again there was a hubbub of voices all wanting to have their say. Karl raised his voice to drown out the muttering.

"Hello. Hello. Hello!" he called, waving his arms in the air.

One by one they fell silent. Karl turned to me.

"What do you say, Björn?"

I took my time, seeing as I knew what he wanted me to say, but I decided to stick to the facts, unlike the rest of them.

"They say there's nothing wrong with me and that I'm perfectly capable of carrying on working."

Several of them looked at me as if they'd only just noticed that I was still there. Hannah with the ponytail and Ann whispered something between them. Several of the others muttered among themselves, like they were still at school.

"Well, surely we can agree . . ." Karl began. "I mean, why don't we say that it's okay as long as Björn doesn't go into the room?"

There was a long silence. Then Jörgen stepped forward. The picture rocked behind him.

"Okay, let's agree on this," he said, fixing his gaze on Karl. "If I see him standing like that once more. Then he's finished. Just saying."

Karl nodded with exaggerated clarity to show that he was really listening. Then he turned to me.

"Do you think you can manage that, Björn?"

I felt a knot in my stomach. But I still opened my mouth and replied.

"Yes."

"Good," Karl said. "So we're all in agreement, then?"

One by one they drifted away.

30.

Late that afternoon the sun peeped out for a couple of minutes. Everyone in the department turned their faces toward the windows, but soon it was gone and shortly afterward it started to snow again.

I kept to my desk and wondered if I ought simply to skip my five-minute breaks and carry on working. Maybe it would be best to shut out everything else in the office and concentrate one hundred percent on work? Maybe Karl and I could come to some arrangement where we calculated how much time I saved by not taking breaks, not chatting with my colleagues, not making private phone calls or running to the toilet every five minutes, like some of the older women did, and reduce the time I spent at work by the same amount?

I took a deep breath and sighed. Getting authorization for something like that seemed unlikely under management that was so hostile to positive developments.

I pulled open the bottom drawer of my desk and put the indoor shoes inside.

. . .

I passed the room twice that day. Once on my way to the toilet, and once when I tidied my desk and went to put two old journals in the recycling bin. I tried not to think about it. I did my best to imitate the others and pretend the room didn't exist. It felt utterly ridiculous. Of course there's a room there, I thought. After all, I can see it. I can touch it. I can feel it. I went round the little corridor once more, as if to check that the door hadn't suddenly disappeared and I'd been imagining it all. But the door was still there. It was firmly fixed in the wall. No question. Solid. As clear as day. It almost made me laugh. I nudged it with my elbow as I walked past it the second time. I heard the sound as the fabric of my jacket touched it. And when all the others were off at lunch, I couldn't see any reason not to go in there for a short while, the tenth time.

31.

After lunch we were all called to yet another meeting in Karl's office. I didn't understand how it could have happened, but I assumed someone must have seen me sneak into the room even though I had taken all reasonable precautions. I prepared myself for the worst.

"Well?" Karl said, when everyone had squeezed into his office.

His gaze swept round the room and settled on Jens. I made an effort to look as relaxed as possible.

"Well . . ." Jens said from over in the corner. "I'd just like to know . . . how much did those shoes cost?"

"The shoes?" Karl said, stretching to his full height.

Jens nodded, with a self-important expression on his face.

"I mean, they weren't free, were they?"

"No," Karl said, picking up a pen which he drummed idly against the edge of the desk. "I took the liberty of—"

Jens didn't let Karl finish his sentence.

"So how daft do you have to behave to get a pair like that?" he went on, to scattered laughter.

Karl gave a strained smile, holding the pen in the air.

"Let's just say that I have a certain amount in the budget for pastoral investment in personnel matters—"

"That's still not fair," Ann said.

"No," Jörgen said.

"This seems to me to be all too typical," Hannah with the ponytail said, folding her arms over her chest. "We didn't get any contribution to the Christmas party. But apparently there's money available now."

"Now listen," Karl said, leaning back in his chair with the pen under his chin. "That's not the same thing."

"So he can turn up and get given stuff just because he acts a bit crazy?" Jörgen said.

Hannah with the ponytail held her arms out.

"It seems to me that it's very unclear what the applicable rules actually are."

Several people nodded.

"The question is," Ann said, "what sort of signals are we sending out?"

When we went back to our places John appeared alongside me. He put his hand on my arm and hissed in my ear: "I saw what you did at lunchtime."

I raised my eyebrows and did my best to look uncomprehending.

"Don't act all innocent," he went on. "I saw you. If I see you again, I'll tell. Just so you know."

32.

The snow carried on falling, and I carried on working. I tried to stick to my fifty-five-minute periods. I even tried smiling. Every time anyone happened to look in my direction I fired off a broad smile, but the whole time I could feel how suspicious everyone else was of me, trying to pretend I wasn't there. Karl came over to our desk. First he chatted with Håkan, then he turned to me. As if everything was normal.

"And how are things with you, then, Björn?"

"What sort of things?" I asked in a neutral voice.

"Well," Karl said, and I could hear how unsettled he was. "What have you spent the last few days doing?"

Naturally he didn't want an answer. He was asking in that pointless way that people do when they ask how you are. They don't want to hear about your health. They just want to hear their own voice, and say things they've said before. They want to make a noise in a social context.

"Why do you want to know?" I said.

"Because I'm your boss," he said.

I looked him in the eye and had a distinct sense of being the stronger person.

"I've initiated a process for developing a set of guiding

principles for the department, identified so-called focus areas, specific targets in various sectors, and gathered a number of criteria. I have chosen to call one of my focus areas 'operations in the center.' "

I clicked to open the document and pointed at the screen.

"I plan to use this to measure the benefit we deliver to customers. To that purpose I have drawn up a questionnaire intended to find out what you customers think about my services."

He looked at me.

"Us customers?"

"I usually think of you as customers."

"What for?"

I allowed myself a gentle sigh.

"Are you really asking me that?"

Karl looked away for a moment and gazed out across the open-plan office. He put his hands on his hips and clenched his jaw. Then he looked at me again.

"Yes, I'm really asking you that," he said.

"I think you maximize your potential better if you imagine a customer at the other end."

I could tell he was impressed even if he was unable to grasp the full extent of the idea and absorb it there and then. I pointed at the screen again.

"So I'd be grateful if you could take the time to fill in

34.

After three days without the room I started to feel unsettled deep down in my gut. I became irritable and noticed I was sweating more than usual. The most acute
abstinence anxiety was starting to subside, but it was as
if the habit was still in my body. I constantly had to stop
myself when I realized my body was on its way there
of its own accord. Like a former smoker fumbling for
a packet of cigarettes. I tried to think about something
else, and every time I felt the urge I tried counting to
twenty.

I didn't go in. I'm sure of that. I sat there clinging to
my desk, thinking that as long as I sat there I was fine.

That night I stood at the window fantasizing about the
room. Remembering details. The mirror, the filing cabinet. The little fan on the desk. I tried to recreate something of the atmosphere in there. But it just felt odd.

this customer questionnaire which you'll find by clicking this link. The survey contains five questions dealing
with the quality of our services, and one question asking if you think any other service should be provided.
The questions are divided according to the various enti-
ties within the Department. Home number. Cell phone
number. Private cell phone number, if applicable, although of course that's voluntary, but I'd be grateful if
you could fill in the questionnaire as fully as possible."

I fell silent and looked at the others. They were all
looking at me now. Håkan was wearing the blue corduroy jacket. It looked streaked somehow. Stained? Karl
had a terribly deep wrinkle above his nose, right between his eyes.

"But Björn," he said. "I asked you to compile a list of
phone numbers, didn't I?"

All my energy slowly drained away. I suddenly had
difficulty concentrating. I felt a chill run down my spine
and a stiffness spread across my neck and shoulders.
Karl disappeared off toward his glass office. Slowly but
surely the others went back to work. Finally even Håkan
turned away, his scruffy corduroy jacket reflecting his
movements like an extra layer of skin.

33.

If it's never happened to you before, it's easy to let your-self be taken in by new acquaintances. You get the impression that they're better than your old ones. You ascribe to them all manner of noble qualities, simply because you don't know them properly.

They might be nice and pleasant the first time, and the second and third. In rare instances also the fourth and fifth. But you will almost always end up disappointed.

Sooner or later you reach a certain point. An occasion when their true self breaks through.

One way of dealing with that sort of thing is simply to assume the worst of people.

Karl, for instance, probably imagines that he means well. He convinces himself that his feeble efforts to help his staff are for the good of all. What he doesn't recognize, or chooses not to recognize, is his own desire to be seen as a hero: the one who solves the problem and gar-ners the praise.

Or Margareta in reception. The appealing exterior, the pleasant demeanor, but before you can say the word "unblemished" she reveals herself to be a junkie.

More people ought to learn to see their worst sides.

Everyone has a bad side. As the poem goes: "What is base in you is also base in them."

On the other hand, it's good to realize that we aren't as remarkable as we might imagine. We want to earn a lot, eat well, and generally have a nice time. Listen to the radio sometimes or watch something on television. Read a book or a journal. We want to have good weather and be able to buy cheap food close to home.

In these terms we are all relatively simple creatures. We dream of finding a more or less pleasant partner, a summer cottage or a time-share on the Costa del Sol. Deep down we just want peace and quiet. A decent dose of easily digested entertainment every now and then.

Anything more is just vain posturing.

35.

The next morning I woke up thinking about the room. I ate my two crispbreads with unsmoked caviar thinking about the room. I walked to work thinking about the room. I was thinking about the room as I passed Margareta in reception, who hadn't looked at me for several weeks now and thus hadn't given me an appropriate opportunity to show that I was keeping my distance. I went up in the lift, got out, and was almost at the door. Very close. I crept toward the forbidden place like a child on Christmas morning. Stopped right next to it. Just stood there, feeling what it felt like to be so close. A bit further down were the three toilets. And beyond them the large recycling bin. There was some writing on it:

Not for cardboard or packaging.

Then I caught sight of Ann at the other end of the corridor. I don't know how she got there but suddenly there she was. Our eyes met and I realized what she was thinking. I shook my head slowly, thinking, "No, it's not what you think."

• • •

"He was there again," she said a short while later when we were both standing in Karl's office.

"I wasn't," I said.

"I saw you."

"No."

"I saw you. You were standing like that again."

"No. I was just standing."

"That's what I'm saying."

"Surely people are allowed to stand still? No one can stop you from just standing for a moment?"

"You were standing on that spot again," Ann said. "You were talking to yourself."

"I was reading. I didn't go inside."

"What were you reading?"

"Not for cardboard or packaging."

"Sorry?" Karl said.

"I didn't go inside," I said.

Karl tried to calm us both down by putting a hand on each of our shoulders. Ann pulled away. She went and stood by the large window facing the office, with her back to us.

"I think it's very unsettling. How's anyone supposed to know if he's there or not? This way we can never be sure."

36.

Word spread from Ann like a group e-mail. During the day practically everyone had passed her desk, and before they walked on they managed to glance in my direction several times. I could see them whispering and making faces.

Some of them talked and pointed at me without any attempt to disguise the fact. A few didn't care if I heard them discussing and diagnosing me. No one replied when I tried to say anything. No one spoke to me at all, apart from Jörgen, who pressed me up against the wall without any warning that afternoon. He held me fairly hard with both hands on my shoulders. His face contorted, his mouth hissing, "You're a freak, you know that?"

I went home slightly early that day because I was unsure of Jörgen's mental state and I was afraid of physical violence. I once got punched in the stomach at primary school, which made me sick and I had to go and see the nurse. The memory brought with it a series of unpleasant associations.

I packed my things in my briefcase and passed reception and Margareta who pretended not to see me again. On the way home I felt I was being watched by a whole load of people. I thought everyone was looking at me. I had to stand at the front of the aisle on the bus because all the seats were taken, so anyone who felt like it could stare at me as much as they wanted. A small child with a pacifier in her mouth stared me right in the eyes for ages. In the end I couldn't help saying:

"Do we know each other?" I got no answer. The little girl just went on sucking the pacifier. Her mother gave me a disapproving stare.

When I got home I leaned my briefcase against the wall. I tried lying down on the bed, but I could feel how tense I was. And scared. It was an unfamiliar feeling, and it upset me. I felt pressure around my ankles and kicked my shoes off onto the floor. The seams of my socks had left marks on my skin.

I got up and turned the television on. I started watching a film with Harrison Ford fighting Russian terrorists. At the end of the film they were fighting by the open loading ramp of a plane while it was in the air, which isn't remotely realistic. So I switched it off and went out into the kitchen instead.

On the radio, an actor was reading a novella he'd written himself. The story included a number, sixty-nine. The actor was claiming that it became ninety-six if you turned it round, which is obviously a total lie, and I suddenly felt how lonely it is, constantly finding yourself the only person who can see the truth in this gullible world.

I turned the radio off and went and stood by the window, looking out. The snow had turned to rain and for a moment I thought it might have leaked into the apartment when I felt the first traces of wetness on my cheeks.

37.

I hadn't cried since primary school, and I didn't like it. It was wet and messy. Crying is for weak people. Crying is a sign of not wanting to pull yourself together, and a way for people of low intelligence to get attention. Crying belongs to small children and onions.

But there was something different about this bout of crying. It was calm, factual crying. Good crying. Water cleansing the tubes, rather like clearing a gutter of leaves and pine needles. A way to get rid of negative energy and make room for something better. It was as if I could feel all the improper thoughts flying away, and new ones taking their place. Better ones. A fresh start.

A new me.

For the first time I realized how oddly I had been behaving. My behavior belonged in the madhouse. And that was where I would end up if I didn't pull myself together.

Thinking about all the stupid things I had done and what they had led to gave me a headache. Going through the various events of the past weeks made me feel distinctly uncomfortable, as I realized how mistaken my behavior had been in a whole series of different situations. I was forced to recognize my limitations, and it pained me.

Still, it was nice being able to think clearly for the first time in ages. And I realized that you have to live and learn.

Whatever doesn't kill you makes you stronger.

Afterward it felt good to have cried. As if I had once again gotten the better of myself and climbed another rung higher on the ladder of my personal development. How high can I get? If I carry on like this, who could possibly stop me?

I could easily have cried a while longer. Obviously I didn't. I sat down at the kitchen table and thought through how to enact my return.

38.

Karl looked up at me as if he'd seen a ghost in fake leather shoes when I went into his office and stood in front of his desk with the new indoor shoes on.

"Why are you late?" he asked.

"I overslept," I said.

Karl raised an eyebrow.

"I'm very sorry," I went on. "I had trouble getting to sleep last night. I lay there thinking. Thinking about recent events. The things I've said and done, and so on. I suddenly seem to get ideas in my head, you see. So I'm lying there thinking about all that. As long as I get enough sleep, I can see it's all nonsense. These past few weeks . . . Then this morning . . . Well, I just had to sort my head out a bit. I've had a lot of new things to try to take in recently."

Karl nodded warily. I took a deep breath and went on.

"I can see that I've been behaving oddly, and I'd like to do what I can to put right any problems I may have caused."

Karl put his pen down on his desk and leaned back in his comfortable office chair.

"Björn, Björn, Björn," he said, as if he were talking to a small child.

"And I understand that my actions have caused problems, not just for me but for you too, and I'd like to ask for your forgiveness. It was never my intention to cause trouble and bad feelings. I promise that from now on there won't be any more of that nonsense."

"Sit down, Björn," Karl said, rolling round to the front of his desk.

I sat down on the uncomfortable little chair. Karl looked at me and I thought I could detect a crooked smile.

"You're an unusual person, Björn. I'm glad you've taken the time to think this through. Maybe it was worth a late start?"

"Obviously, I'll make up the time I've lost . . ." I began, but Karl gestured dismissively with his hand.

"Don't worry about that, Björn. If we can get you sorted out, then this little break will have been entirely justified."

He looked at my new indoor shoes and lit up. It was obvious that he liked what he saw.

"They're really nice," I said.

"Aren't they?" Karl said with a smile.

"Yes, that's what I just said," I said.

He cleared his throat and turned serious again.

"So are we agreed on the rules now, Björn?"

"Yes," I said.

He leaned toward me.

"And can we forget all about that room now?"

"Of course," I said.

He looked at me and I realized that I ought to nod. I nodded.

"Good," he said, and rolled back to the other side of the desk. "Good, Björn. No one will be happier than me if we can find a solution to this."

"I'm pleased," I said.

"Yes," Karl said, and smiled again.

39.

On my way to my workstation I tried to find someone to say hello to, but no one looked at me. Håkan was leafing through some papers and humming to himself. I sat down at my desk and switched the computer on.

Half an hour later I handed in a printout of the updated list of phone numbers. Karl raised his head and brightened up.

"Excellent," he said.

He scratched his head and looked around, as if he were thinking. I stood in the doorway and waited. Most of the staff in the department had gone home for the day. I thought I might as well stay a bit longer.

"Do you know what?" he said after a few moments. "Tomorrow, could you put together a list of which projects have been quality assured and which ones haven't? It would be good to have it on paper."

I nodded.

"You'll be able to tell from where they've come from if they've been checked or not."

"Of course," I said.

I returned to my place and sat down just as Håkan

got up, put some documents in his bag, slung it over his corduroy jacket, and disappeared without a word to me.

I logged in and got to work at once.

An hour or so later I decided to call it a day and go home too. I was almost on my own in the office. I turned the lamp off, gathered my coat and briefcase, went out to the lift, and went straight down to reception. Without passing the room.

40.

I slept relatively well that night. I slept the sleep that only someone who has been down at the bottom but is now on his way back up can sleep. The sleep of someone who recognizes that an inferior position is a good position to attack from. The sleep of someone with a plan.

41.

You don't turn a river by abruptly trying to get it to change direction. You don't have that much power. No matter how strong you are. The river will just overwhelm you and obstinately carry on pretty much as before. You can't make it change direction overnight. No one can. On the contrary, you have to start by flowing with it.

You have to capture its own force and then slowly but surely lead it in the desired direction. The river won't notice it's being led if the curve is gentle enough. On the contrary, it will think it's flowing just the same as usual, seeing as nothing seems to have changed.

42.

Uneventful days. Days without any particular character. Days which at first glance didn't appear to have led to much. Days that no one pays any attention to. Every day there came more and more documents from the investigators on the sixth and seventh floors, all of them waiting to be turned into framework decisions.

Håkan was becoming more and more anxious about the workload. He started making excuses. Moaning about the quality of the investigations. Their layout, content, incoherent argumentation.

So you're the only one who's perfect? I thought. How ironic.

Håkan and Karl had endless heated discussions that always ended with talk about the possibility of the entire Authority being closed down.

The threat of closure hung like an evil spirit over the whole department. Probably the whole Authority. I assumed this was the government's way of keeping us on our toes and not letting anyone think they were safe. But Håkan was irritated at the investigators and the work they did most of the time. He waved documents at Karl when he walked past:

"How am I supposed to formulate a clear, easily

understood text from this rubbish? Do they even know what decision they've come to themselves?"

I went in to see Karl with money for the indoor shoes. At first he didn't want to take it, but I insisted, and explained that I would have bought a pair exactly like them if I'd gotten them myself. After a while he relented. He took the money and put it in his own pocket. I didn't say anything.

43.

Later that day Karl came over to see Håkan, and I heard them discussing the formulation of a new decision. I took care not to look up from my work as I listened to them talking.

Håkan was groaning and constantly scratching his sideburns, and said he couldn't produce a clearer text from that material, and that it was impossible to work any faster, particularly at the moment when there wasn't exactly a calm atmosphere conducive to work.

Without looking at them I could tell that this last remark was aimed at me, and I thought I could feel them both glancing in my direction. I pretended not to notice.

Soon I had finished my task. Sorting out the quality-assured projects was really just a matter of checking the signatures at the end of each file. One investigator meant no. Two or more control declarations with different save dates meant yes.

I was done just before lunch and another printout was delivered to Karl's office. Karl thanked me and smiled, but I could see how tired he was.

"What shall I do now?" I asked.

Karl looked at me as if he had no idea what I was talking about. He stared blindly through the window facing the office.

"Well . . ." he muttered, sighing through his nose.

"Perhaps there's some text that . . . ?"

Karl looked at me.

"What are you thinking?"

"No, I was just wondering if I could help . . ."

"No thanks, Björn. I don't think so. It'll be fine. But you could . . ."

He looked round the room.

". . . check all the printers . . . make sure they've all got enough paper and so on."

We looked at one another, both of us aware of the menial task he was asking a civil servant to do, and I realized that my humiliation had to be dragged right down to the very bottom. I didn't mind. I was prepared. I nodded and went out to find some photocopy paper.

All the printers in the department ended up as full of paper as they possibly could be without the paper feed jamming, or the thin plastic holding it being so overburdened that it broke.

When I saw several of the others having a coffee

break I went over to the little kitchen as well and got myself a cup.

A peculiar silence spread round the small room. They all drank their coffee, but the easy banter was missing. I tried to avoid making eye contact with Jörgen, who still looked likely to have an outburst at any moment. All you could hear was the sound of my spoon stirring the cup.

44.

When I returned to my place I saw that the inevitable had now happened. Håkan's papers had finally overflowed onto my desk.

Håkan's chair was empty but his desk was covered with files and documents, all waiting to be formulated into new framework decisions. Several piles of printouts were positioned so that they were almost nudging the back of my computer screen.

I felt a pang of my old intolerance. A gust of my old self who had been far too excitable, too guileless in purely tactical terms.

I sat down at my desk and put my hands against all his things. Then I simply pushed them back until everything was just inside the edge of his desktop. I heard one or two things fall to the floor on the other side of the desk.

When Håkan came back with a large pile of papers in his arms he didn't even bother trying to make room among the mess on his desk, but impudently parked it all on my side. He leaned down and picked up the papers that had ended up on the floor. He didn't even seem to wonder how they had gotten there.

Soon he disappeared again.

My initial impulse was of course to repeat my earlier procedure and this time push everything a bit further to make him realize what he was doing. But then my eyes were caught by one of the printouts. *Investigation. Case 1,636*, it said. I realized that this was an opportunity. Without even asking for it, I had been given a helping hand. An almost meditative calm spread through me.

I looked around. I took hold of the pile of papers with both hands and put what had been left on my desk in my drawer.

45.

Håkan spent a large part of the afternoon trying in vain to find the missing investigations. Even if he didn't say anything, I knew that was what he was doing. He picked up books and files, looked underneath things, muttering to himself and occasionally swearing quietly.

I watched him go in to see Karl, gesticulating with his arms. Karl looked sweatier than ever. At some point Håkan gestured in my direction, but Karl merely shook his head.

I took care to participate in all the group coffee breaks and idle conversations. No one spoke to me or even looked at me, but I was there. I was taking part. I was a physical presence among them.

To start with, I noticed that everything would stop as soon as I came along. I would stand beside the others and pretend I hadn't noticed. In the end, I came to assume the role of passive participant, the person no one bothers about, but whose presence is a precondition for the general character of social interaction.

• • •

By five o'clock most of the others had left, but I stayed behind as usual. I did an extra circuit of all the printers and checked that they were all full, mostly to make sure that the others had all gone home.

Then I went back to my desk. I opened the drawer and took out the top bundle of papers.

Investigation. Case 1,636

I put it in my briefcase, put my coat on to leave, checked once more that there was no one left, crept round to the corridor with the toilets, turned the light on, and slipped inside the room for the eleventh time.

46.

The fluorescent light flickered and clicked inside the room like a hot tin roof in the summer. It was quiet and cool. The desktop fan, with its rotating blades inside a stainless steel mesh, lent the room an almost foreign feeling. It wasn't new, but it had been extremely well maintained. Classy. Un-Swedish.

It was easy to think of bygone times in the room. A whole series of eminent decision makers behind the perfect desk.

It felt indescribably good to be back inside this small space again. I stood there for a long time just enjoying it. Resting one hand gently on the desk.

The desktop felt completely smooth under my fingertips. You could probably rest your cheek on it if you felt like it. I didn't. I pulled out the comfortable office chair, sat down, my back straight, and read through the entire bundle of papers.

It was surprisingly simple. Words and formulations that would otherwise take a long time to grasp flowed into my consciousness in a perfectly natural way. I understood at once.

Most of it seemed obvious. As if someone had asked

me to fill in the right answers in a third-grade math book.

I looked up at the ceiling and tried to memorize a few keywords. As I was resting my eyes on the red painting with its plain motif I formulated a couple of simple phrases in my head. I realized at once that they worked well. Simple and clear.

I leafed back and forth through the material. It was clumsily expressed. I had to agree with Håkan on that. Some sections were completely unfocused, but could clearly be formulated the way I had just tried out. It was as if I had cleaned the document in order to reveal its pure lines.

Now that I knew how it ought to be expressed, it struck me as odd that no one had thought of it before. Had I missed something? Was there something I didn't understand? Or was it really this simple?

47.

"Excellent!" Karl exclaimed as he came over and slapped Håkan on the back with the palm of his hand the following day.

Håkan turned round, looked at Karl, and raised his eyebrows lazily.

"What?"

Karl smacked 1,636 down on the desktop. Håkan leaned over and read.

"This is exactly what I meant," Karl said. "This is brilliant, Håkan. Bloody hell, it's genius! Factual and concise. No room for misunderstanding."

It was clear that he was in an extremely good mood. His whole face was beaming. Håkan turned to Karl.

"That isn't mine," he said bluntly.

Karl's joy was interrupted and he frowned. He picked up the document and pulled his glasses down, perched them on his nose, and looked at the number: 1,636.

"What?"

"This isn't mine."

"Of course it's yours. I gave it to you."

"Okay," Håkan said. "But I didn't write that."

Karl pushed his glasses up onto his forehead again.

"What do you mean, you didn't write it?"

"Someone else must have written it," Håkan said.

He turned back to what he was doing, leaving Karl holding 1,636 in his hand, a mass of furrows on his brow.

"But . . ." Karl began.

He went back inside his office and I saw him sit in there, inspecting the document from all angles, all the while with that bewildered look on his face.

That afternoon Karl called Ann and John into his office. I watched him show them my printout, but they both shook their heads. It was actually rather a shame, I thought. If one of them had falsely taken the credit for my work, the situation would have been even better. We would have been able to increase the bounce of my trampoline, so to speak. But evidently neither of them was brazen enough. I would have to carry on as planned.

Just before I went to lunch I felt I needed to go to the toilet. I took the long route past the lift so that everyone would clearly see that I was avoiding the room. When I came out again I took the same route back, passing several of my colleagues on their way to the lift. They could all see that I was coming from the toilet. I passed the door of the room as if it didn't exist.

48.

When the working day was over and everyone had gone home, I smuggled the next investigation into my briefcase, closed it firmly, and snuck into the room.

I unpacked my things on the magnificent desk and started work on 1,842.

As soon as I emerged I wrote a couple of short sentences in my notepad so I didn't forget my train of thought in there. I sat down at my computer and wrote up the text. The whole process went much quicker today. It was like I'd learned something about the way things fit together. Something about the way time and space interact.

I went over to Karl's office, opened the glass door, and put the document on his desk just after half past ten in the evening.

49.

The next day I repeated the process with case 1,199, the only difference being that I took the neatly typed document home with me overnight.

The next morning I went into Karl's office before he got in, making sure that Ann witnessed it. I could clearly see how watchful she became the moment I entered Karl's little glass cube. She stared at me as I left the document on his desk. And just after Karl had arrived and hung up his outdoor clothes on the hanger, sure enough, she was there telling tales.

I couldn't have arranged it better.

50.

"Ann tells me you're the person who left this on my desk?" Karl said, holding up framework decision 1,199.

I nodded.

"Who wrote it?"

"I did."

He stood there for a while, just looking at me without saying anything. As if he were trying to work out whether or not I was telling the truth. He cleared his throat and scratched an ear lobe.

"You did?"

I nodded again, and couldn't help noticing that Håkan was suddenly listening.

"Who . . . who asked you to do it?" Karl said.

I raised my eyebrows and answered slowly.

"I took it for granted that it was my duty, seeing as the files were on my desk."

"The files were on your desk?"

"Yes."

"Who put them there?" Karl said, glancing at Håkan, who quickly looked down and pretended to be reading his papers.

"I've no idea," I said. "I assumed—"

"Please, come with me."

He led the way toward the little glass box without waiting for me. I looked at Håkan, who was still pretending not to have noticed anything, but his neck was bright red. I got up and walked very slowly after Karl into his office. Karl sat down behind his desk.

"Close the door," he said.

I did as he said and tried to adopt a concerned expression, as if I were expecting another reprimand for something. There was a certain pleasure in playing the innocent schoolboy, seeing as I knew what was coming. Karl fixed his eyes on me.

"Björn, what's going on here?"

"I'm sorry if I've caused any trouble. I didn't mean to take someone else's work. I was just convinced I was meant to do it because the case notes were on my desk and . . ."

"Can you tell me who wrote 1,842 and . . . let's see, 1,636?"

"I did."

"Björn, I hope you are aware that all of us in this department . . . we always stick to the truth."

"That is the truth."

Karl spun his chair slightly and stroked his chin with his fingers. He picked up the documents and seemed almost to be weighing them in his hand.

"The DG is very pleased," he said out of nowhere.

"Oh?" I said, trying to look surprised.

"He says we've finally got the right tone. That these texts you've written ought to be the template for all future framework decisions in the communal sector."

51.

I looked at the picture Jörgen usually leaned against when we had meetings here in Karl's office and tried to enjoy the moment when the new order here at the Authority slowly began to take shape. The picture was of some appetizing-looking fruit. You could almost have believed it was real. I came to think of an artist who could draw an empty sheet of paper and make you think it was a real piece of paper, so you'd go up to it wondering why someone had put an empty sheet of paper in a glass frame, but then you'd discover that it was a drawing, like an optical illusion. Quite funny, actually.

The thought made me smile.

"I didn't know . . ." Karl said, and I could see he was having severe difficulty coming to terms with the idea of me as a leading light in this field. He had regarded me as a nothing, an encumbrance, someone who needed to be watched and looked after. Now that he'd made his bed he was having to lie in it.

He looked up at me and smiled, clearly uncertain about how to treat me. It was like there was something inside him that was still fighting against the idea. I could easily draw this out a bit longer, I thought. Let him squash me even further down. I could exploit my lowly status and make the turnaround even greater, even more of a shock.

But this was where we were. At last he had realized, and maybe I ought to have been pleased that he was at least intelligent enough to recognize talent when he saw it. That isn't always the case.

"You surprise . . ." he went on, waving my texts.

I stayed quiet. And smiled. Knowing when to keep your mouth shut is an art.

"If you could imagine carrying on . . . that you might be able to take on some more . . ."

I cleared my throat and frowned gently. Taking my time.

"I'd be happy to help in any way I can," I said, "but bearing in mind my other duties . . ."

I glanced toward the photocopier and Karl took the hint.

"We can sort that out, Björn."

"I just mean that it might be difficult finding the time to look after the printers and . . ."

"Obviously, you wouldn't have to do anything of that sort . . ."

"And the quality assurances . . ."

Karl raised his voice slightly to indicate that he was serious. That all that sort of nonsense was at an end now.

"I'm sorry, Björn, if I underestimated you . . ."

He got up from his chair and I could see the tension in his face as he steeled himself to say what was coming. I smiled and waited.

". . . but it isn't always easy to see the skills of all your colleagues. Especially not . . ."

He fell silent and sat down on the edge of the desk. He looked tired. He sighed and ran his hand over his hair.

"I apologize, Björn. There's been a lot going on recently."

"Apology accepted," I said, and made myself comfortable in his office chair.

He looked down at me with his mouth wide open. I leaned back and folded my hands over my stomach.

"Would you like to talk about it?" I said.

52.

The following morning I was able to run my finger slowly over the numbers on the cover of my first framework decision, which now had its own reference number: 16c36/1.

I had gone down to reception and asked for it the day it became publicly accessible. I could smell the fresh ink, and I let Margareta behind the counter get a glimpse of the case manager's name on the flyleaf. You could have been a part of all this, I thought. But drugs got in the way.

"How are things going for you these days?" she asked after a pause.

I didn't answer. I didn't even look at her. I had decided to regard her as a stranger, a complete unknown. And neither condone nor condemn what she did in her own time.

53.

Rumors of my success swept through the whole department like a wave. Someone had heard and carried the news to the rest of the group. I saw Hannah with the ponytail talking to Karin outside the kitchen, and via Karin I was able to follow the path of the news to John and the gang in the section for the financing of inspection visits. After a while almost the whole of Supervision stood up, talking to each other and looking in my direction. I tried to read their reactions, but it was difficult as I was constantly having to pretend I hadn't noticed and was preoccupied with my work.

In fact things were relatively stress free, and I didn't have to rush my fifty-five-minute periods seeing as the most concentrated part, the actual formulation itself, always happened inside the room. In the evenings and at night.

One day when Håkan got back from a coffee break I noticed that even he had been hosed down by the torrent of information about the new star in the office. He smiled when he asked but I could see the icy chill in his eyes.

"So how long were you planning on keeping your talent hidden, then?" he said.

I didn't answer. He had a large white patch on one shoulder and going part way down his chest. Hadn't he noticed? It looked scruffy.

"Do you think it's funny going round pretending to be unstable, just so you can show everyone your tightrope routine later on?"

I said nothing. I recognized the nature of his questions. They were rhetorical. It's always best to ignore those. Treat them like they don't exist. But the stain was real.

"Don't you think you should go and change your shirt?" I asked after a while, nodding toward the stain.

Håkan glanced sullenly down at his shoulder. Then he hissed through gritted teeth:

"When did you take those files?"

I adopted a questioning look that I had practiced at home in front of the mirror. I thought it gave the desired impression.

John caught up with me on the way to the kitchen. He held out his hand.

"Congratulations, Björn," he said with a crooked smile. "It's great that things are going so well for you now."

I took his hand and thanked him.

"I'm sorry about all that business before," he said.

"You know how things get in stressful workplaces. There isn't always enough time to talk things through calmly."

I decided to hold back from responding and just gave him a quizzical look.

"I mean, places like this aren't exactly famous for taking care of their staff when they get a bit—well, how can I put it?—overwrought."

I went on looking at him in silence. It was obvious that it was starting to make him nervous.

"But I'm really pleased you're back on track, Björn. I just wanted you to know. Even the DG is pleased. He's let us know how happy he is."

He let out one of those exaggerated laughs, as if he was hoping I'd join in. I didn't. His laughter died out. He looked round, leaned forward, and said in a confidential tone:

"Even the Minister is said to be pleased with our recent progress. You might manage to save all our jobs."

He patted me on the shoulder and walked off.

54.

I worked on the investigations in the room in the evenings and at night. I edited them during the day and found every part of the job as good as you might expect when it's done by an expert. Inside the room, I found a structure for the work. I regarded the investigator's words as gospel, and through a process of elimination all that remained in the end was a clear and unambiguous decision. I found it easy.

Obviously each and every individual has different ways of reaching a decision. Some people find it hard, or think it feels strange. I discovered that I find it very easy to make decisions. It seemed to come naturally. I'm happy to decide things, and every time it felt perfectly fine formulating the way that things should be.

Jens came up to me one day fishing for advice.

"How come you can suddenly ... ?" Jens said. "I mean ... we had no idea ..."

"Hard work," I said. "Hard work is the father of success."

"But how do you go about it, exactly?"

I smiled.

"I'm sure you can understand that I can't reveal my reasoning. That would be both undesirable and impossible. The best thing for the department and for you personally would be for you to work out your own way of reasoning on your own."

55.

To start with I only dealt with four-figure cases. But as news of my success began to spread, the occasional three-figure case would land on my desk. Suddenly Karl came up to me, all excited, and asked how I would feel about taking on number 97. It was a direct request from the DG, he said. I said I'd be happy to. Framework decision number 97 was my first double-digit case.

Karl came with me up to the investigators to pick up the material. We could have done with a cart. As he walked beside me along the corridors of the upper floors with the heavy burden in his arms, it almost felt like he was my assistant. In some ways he had started to rely on me. I remember thinking: This is your future, Karl. Stick close to me.

Jörgen was losing his temper more and more often. Every now and then one of his outbursts would be aimed at Karl, usually for no obvious reason. But Karl shouted back, which I thought reasonable. Angry dogs need to be kept on a short leash.

56.

My days were spent writing up and editing, but seeing as that didn't fill the whole working day I soon abandoned my fifty-five-minute method and had a lot of time left over for networking in the office.

I spent long periods by the coffee machine in the little kitchen, and noticed how people's attitudes toward me gradually changed. I was given the space to spread out in social conversation. I would declare my opinion on various subjects and could immediately identify those who agreed with me, and those who said they did but were lying.

One day when we were standing there, Hannah with the ponytail suddenly said: "It's great that you changed the bulb in here, Jens. It was high time that got done."

She was grinning broadly and Jens tried to look nonchalant.

"Oh, it's no big deal," he said.

I put my cup down.

"I thought about doing that a few weeks ago," I said.

And suddenly I realized the difference between me and my colleagues. I was ahead of them the whole time. By about two weeks. It took them numerous attempts to understand what I could see at the first go. Was it the same thing with the room? Would they stand there one day and discover what I had tried to show them such a long time before? Maybe they were just too immature to see what seemed utterly obvious to me? Was this how Copernicus felt?

57.

As the days passed, I began to feel a degree of irritation spread out and take hold of me.

Karl always helped me with heavy piles of documents. Sometimes he would be wholly responsible for their transportation from the investigators down to our department, if I had a lot to do, for instance. But when the work actually had to be done, I had to shift the heaps of material into the room without anyone seeing. It started to get rather wearing after a while.

Eventually I began to feel irritated at having to keep quiet about my real workplace. Besides, I was finding it both uncomfortable and tiring to have to wait until all the others had left each day before I could get any real work done.

Everyone else in the department carried on as usual. Took their breaks, chatted. Which annoyed me as well.

I realized fairly early on that there was a difference between my time and other people's. I don't just do one thing at a time. I can be on my way somewhere, but I'll spend the time thinking about other things, things that may not have anything to do with what I'm doing just then. That way I maximize the use of my time.

For instance, I don't just stand on the bus staring out of the window at things I've seen hundreds of times. I think about other things instead, calculating and thinking things through. Making decisions.

You have to apply the same principle in dealing with other people. Otherwise certain conversations can become incredibly time-consuming. I listen until I realize where the conversation is going, which in many cases can be deduced fairly early on, then I switch off and concentrate on other things. There's no reason to hear the same thing twice. Or three or four times. Ordinary people listen to a huge amount of nonsense that they would be better off without.

Ordinary people can do one thing at a time. I can deal with plenty. Surely I ought to be rewarded for that?

58.

"If it's possible, I'd like to go through a few practical issues," I said to Karl in his office a couple of days later.

"Shut the door, Björn," Karl said, parking his little cart in the corner behind the desk.

I had asked for a private meeting to go through a list of things I couldn't help thinking about. Maybe I could put a bit of pressure on him now that I had established myself and become more or less indispensable.

Karl was sweating a lot, and I couldn't help wondering deep down about the state of his health.

"I noticed that I didn't get an e-mail about the staff-development days," I said.

"Didn't you get the e-mail?" he said with a look of surprise between breaths.

"Well, that depends on your definition."

"How do you mean?"

"Well," I said, leaning back in the chair. "It wasn't addressed to me."

"But you got the e-mail?"

"I was copied into it, yes. I'd appreciate it if my name could be included in the list of recipients. As it is, I just got it as a copy."

Karl pulled a handkerchief from his trouser pocket and mopped his brow.

"But you did get the e-mail?"

"Only as a copy."

"Do you want to attend the staff-development days? If you do, I can just—"

I shook my head.

"I'd never consider that," I said.

We both sat there in silence as he folded the handkerchief and put it back in his pocket.

"Obviously, I'm not making any demands," I said. "I just wanted you to know that you'd be making it easier for me to choose all of you here, if there was ever any chance of my considering anything else."

"Considering anything else, Björn?"

"You never know."

"Are you thinking of leaving us?"

"I can't go into that."

Karl rubbed his head with one hand. I thought I could see a stiff smile on his lips.

"Well, go ahead. What would you like to see?"

I took out the pad on which I'd written a few reminders.

"Jörgen has to go."

Karl looked at me, wide-eyed.

"Sorry?"

"I want Jörgen to leave. Be removed from the department. He can stay in the building, just out of my sight and hearing."

"Björn, that sort of demand—"

"And I'm sure," I went on, "that my suggestions are well within the bounds of the organization's wishes."

"What . . . what did you say?"

"I think you probably heard what I said."

He patted his legs and attempted a strained grin.

"You don't understand, Björn. That isn't how it works. I can't just dismiss someone who—"

"I think you can. With a bit of imagination."

Karl shook his head. He looked at me, then shook his head again.

"Like I said," I continued. "Obviously I can't decide what happens to anyone else . . ."

"No, exactly," Karl said.

". . . apart from myself."

He looked at me, suddenly serious.

"I see. What else?"

I took my time, crossing one leg over the other. I adjusted my jacket with a pointed gesture.

"Håkan should be demoted."

Karl held up a hand to stop me, but I carried on before he had time to interrupt.

"That can be motivated by disciplinary measures. I'll see that you get the necessary evidence."

"You don't understand," Karl began again.

"What don't I understand?"

"Björn—"

"According to the DG, I'm the only person in the department who's understood—"

"Björn, we can't just suddenly—"

"Do you want to hear my demands or not?"

Karl stared at me as if he were hoping I was going to stop joking. But I wasn't joking. I was deadly serious.

"Håkan has a wife and children . . ."

"I can't take that into consideration."

Karl shook his head again, let out a deep breath, and looked very unhappy.

"What else?"

"Last but not least," I said. "Possibly more important than everything else."

"Yes?" Karl said.

"I need free access to the room."

Karl was staring again, and I thought I could see one of his eyebrows twitch.

"You mean, 'the room'?"

I nodded.

"No!" Karl said emphatically.

He stood up and started pacing.

"No, no, no, Björn," he went on. "I thought we were done with that room?"

"Not exactly," I said.

59.

"For God's sake, there is no room!" Jörgen said, waving his arms about and making the fruit picture sway.

He was sweating and looked like he might lose control at any moment. I thought this ought to be enough to make even Karl realize that keeping him in the department was untenable.

When we were all gathered like this it was called a big departmental meeting, but it just felt like Karl's little glass cube was getting smaller and smaller. And hotter and hotter.

Yet there was something of a different atmosphere this time. Some people, John, for instance, were sticking closer to me.

"But there is no room," Jörgen almost hissed this time. "Is there?"

He was staring at Karl almost beseechingly. Karl held up his hand.

"Perhaps we could agree on the formulation 'the room does not exist for everyone'?"

"What the hell are you talking—" Jörgen began, but Karl interrupted him.

"I'm just trying to find a phrase that works for all of us. Can we agree . . . ?"

"But there is no room!"

Jörgen was getting close now. Jens hurriedly added:

"First there was the business with the shoes . . ."

"I've paid for them," I said.

". . . and now this."

"Either it's there or it isn't!" Jörgen practically yelled.

John suddenly stood up beside me.

"Maybe we've reached a point now where the room has a certain significance. And on those terms then it obviously does exist."

Everyone looked at John.

"Either there is a room there, or there isn't," Ann said.

"It's not quite that simple," Karl said.

"Isn't it? So what the hell is it, then?" Jens said, glaring at Karl.

Karl turned to me. I cleared my throat, ran one finger over my chin, and made no effort to hurry.

"To put it mildly," I began, "we can probably take it for granted that out of everyone here, I'm the one who makes the largest contribution, purely in terms of work. I have to say that it seems more than reasonable for me to have access to a space of my own, and the room is a place where I feel I can work."

Håkan was staring at me open-mouthed, then said:

"But it doesn't exist?"

Karl looked round.

"I wonder," he said, "if it might be a good idea to bring in a consultant to look at this issue."

"What would the consultant do?" Niklas said.

"It might help us find a new way of looking at things."

Jörgen craned his neck toward Karl. He was making an effort not to lose his grip.

"You're going to bring in a consultant to tell us the room doesn't exist?"

"Or does exist," I said. "I can quite understand that you might be scared of bringing in an outsider."

"That costs money," Ann said.

"Maybe it would be worth it?" Karl said.

Suddenly there was a loud noise. Not a howl, but an almost muffled sound. It was Jörgen.

"Jörgen."

"I think I'm going mad," Jörgen said.

"Okay, you need to calm down," Karl said. "It's extremely important that we do the right thing in a situation like this. It's important for the whole Authority. We're not going to make any hasty decisions."

I got the impression that he glanced in my direction. I stood up and walked toward the door.

"Call me when you've finished working out how to clear up this elaborate charade. I'm perfectly prepared to overlook the whole thing and move on, but I'd like you to identify one person responsible for it. Someone I can consider as—how can I put it?—the guilty party. Have you got that?"

No one said anything. Their mouths were all hanging open. Even Jörgen was sitting there gawking.

Karin looked very unhappy.

"Can't we say that the room exists a little bit?"

Hannah with the ponytail tilted her head to one side.

"It strikes me that it would feel rather uncomfortable to have a room that only Björn is allowed inside."

While everyone was looking at her I walked out. I heard the discussion resume with fresh impetus as soon as I closed the door.

60.

I sat at my desk, moving the mouse up and down over the mouse pad. All the while I could see above my screen the heated debate taking place inside Karl's office. It looked quite funny, all those big people in such a little room. It was like they were part of some work of art. They were gesticulating and talking. I heard fragments of sentences, "a monster" and "ought to get help," but also "remember that Björn is working on two-figure cases these days."

Eventually things quieted down and I stretched to get a better view of what they were up to.

After a good while they all emerged.

John came straight over to me. The others followed him, stumbling rather aimlessly, like the flock of sheep that they actually were. No one really seemed to know where to go. No one seemed capable of going back to work.

"What's going on?" I asked.

"Karl's on his way up to the DG," John said.

"Oh, what for?"

"He's going to ask him."

"About what?"

"About the room. That's what we agreed. That this is a matter for the DG."

I smiled and patted him on the shoulder.

"That's probably right," I said.

Ann came up to us, and behind her trailed the rest of them. They ended up in a circle around Håkan's and my desks. As if they didn't really know where to go. As if I were going to read them a story.

"What exactly is it that you want?" Ann asked me.

She looked distraught. Unhappy. I wondered if she was about to burst into tears. I tried to answer in a gentle, friendly tone of voice.

"I just want to do my job," I said.

There was muttering in the congregation.

"And what do you think we're doing, Björn?"

That was Håkan's voice. He was having trouble getting to his place with everyone crowding round my desk. I looked up. First at him. Then at all the other anxious pairs of eyes around me.

"Obviously I don't know with one hundred percent certainty," I said. "I can only speak for myself. Seeing as I have noticed the room over there and find a certain joy in working there, I have no option but to accept its existence, as I'm sure you can understand. I could work on the assumption that I myself am wrong and the rest of you right, but that doesn't make much sense in my head. I simply have to assume that one of us is lying. Because I know that I am telling the truth, I draw the conclusion that the rest of you are telling untruths. That's simply the logical conclusion."

I saw several of them lower their gaze. Ann looked nervous. Jörgen was sweating.

"What I can't help wondering is whether you've done this before? As well as which of you are involved, and how you managed the practicalities? When did you decide? At what level has this been authorized? For instance, I don't imagine that the DG has been informed about this, which is odd, seeing as you must surely all recognize that if something like this got out, it would mean the end for the whole department?"

Håkan looked at me with horror in his eyes and I had time to think: Now you get it!

"In some ways it's such a grandiose and detailed project," I went on, "and so ingeniously malicious that I can't help being rather fascinated."

I leaned forward and rested my elbows on the desk.

"It's going to be very exciting to hear what the DG has to say when Karl comes back down. Taking the DG's decision as my starting point, I am going to have to resolve how we proceed with all this. Who among you will be staying, and who will have to leave."

I saw from the clock that it had gone half past eleven and I could feel my stomach starting to rumble gently.

"The very least I can ask is that you agree to nominate one person who can take the time to go through exactly how it all worked with me: what important decisions were taken, who was the driving force behind it, who was in favor or opposed to it, and so on. That person must also be prepared to accept severe punishment and leave the organization immediately. I suggest that you discuss this among yourselves and come back to me once you've decided upon a suitable candidate."

I gathered my things together on the desk. I put on my coat and went off to lunch early.

On the way out I went straight to the door in the corridor, opened it, and stepped inside. I stood there for a good while, thinking:

Soon you'll be mine.

61.

As soon as I returned from lunch Margareta in reception informed me that a meeting was about to start. I had treated myself to some sushi from the little restaurant just across the street from the big, redbrick building. I had sat there eating my raw fish and looking out across the square with its incomprehensible sculptures. I took my time, and was well aware that I was slightly late as I climbed up the flight of gray steps leading to the Authority.

"They're waiting in Karl's office," Margareta said.

As usual, I thought, and took the lift up. I went into the glass cubicle and tried to get a glimpse of Karl. The whole department had been summoned and everyone had dutifully trotted into his office, but Karl wasn't there yet. This was starting to feel like a habit. Håkan in his blue jacket.

Håkan was pinching the bridge of his nose with his thumb and forefinger. He was leaning against the desk where Karl usually stood, and he looked at me wearily. I started to get an idea of what this was about, and tried to work out who among the staff had been telling tales and thus indirectly brought about this improvised meeting. Without Karl. From past experience it seemed most likely to have been Ann. She went and stood beside Håkan when I walked in, ready—responsible, somehow. With a look on her face that wasn't entirely dissatisfied.

Don't they ever get fed up? I thought, and let out a small sigh.

"Ann, you had something to say to us?" Håkan began, like a sort of stand-in boss.

"Yes," she said, tilting her chin.

"Aren't we going to wait for Karl?" I said.

Håkan shook his head firmly.

"No need," he said. "Well, what did you want to say, Ann?"

Ann stretched and took a deep breath.

"Björn was standing there again."

A murmur went round the room. One of those "oohs" you sometimes hear in American sitcoms when the audience reacts obediently to something cute said by a child. But there was nothing cute about this. This was an expression of "What did we say?" and "Knew it! He's done it again!"

"And this time I've got witnesses," Ann said.

The loaded atmosphere in there, their infernal obstinacy and united front made my cup run over. I could hear that I was speaking louder than necessary when I was no longer able to hold back the torrent of frustration growing inside me.

"That's absolutely true, my friends," I said. "I have made use of the room for all manner of activities. I have gone there on a daily basis in recent weeks. I have done most of my—and forgive me for putting it like this— singularly successful work in there, during the evenings and at night. And yes, I intend to carry on doing so."

I went round the desk that Håkan and Ann were leaning against and sat down on Karl's very comfortable office chair. The others looked at me.

"That's enough now. More than enough. You have just obliged me to meet force with force. I have no other option but to put myself up against you all."

There was total silence in the room. You could have heard a pin drop.

"There are a couple of you that I could imagine reaching an accommodation with. You, John, have shown a degree of loyalty. And that will obviously be rewarded. The rest of you can start packing your things, because from now on the following applies: I will only stay on the condition that you go."

I leaned back calmly in the chair.

"Now, I suggest that we wait for the DG's decision."

62.

Five, six, maybe seven minutes of intense silence passed inside Karl's office without anyone so much as moving a finger. No one could think of anything to say or do. It was like everyone was holding their breath. Finally Karl came rushing in, in a very undignified manner, breathless and with beads of sweat on his forehead.

"Hello, everyone. I've come straight from the DG. We spent a long time talking. I informed him about everything . . . well, everything that has happened, and our various different opinions about . . . and I can tell you that . . ."

He paused and looked at me, slightly uncertain. Maybe in an attempt to gauge my reaction in advance, maybe to be sure he still had me with him. He went on slowly and clearly:

". . . the DG and I have had a . . . conversation . . . about the room. By which I mean, its existence or otherwise, and so on."

The entire room was utterly silent. Karl cleared his throat. I saw Håkan swallow, and Jörgen loosened his tie slightly.

"The DG has shown me the plans. He was in no

doubt. Very—how shall I put it?—persuasive in his argument."

He blinked and cleared his throat again as he turned toward the others.

"The DG says that on this, the fourth floor, between the lift and the three toilets . . . there is absolutely no other space."

63.

I remained seated in Karl's chair for a while as all the others filed out and drifted back to their workstations. Slowly but surely the office resumed its usual atmosphere. As if nothing had happened.

I was trying to work out if the DG could possibly be involved in this conspiracy, or if Karl was simply lying. How could I check? I got up carefully, wondering if I ought to pay a visit of my own to the Director General.

When I came out of the office I saw that plastic tape had been set up between the walls by the lift and at the other end of the corridor. Karl came after me.

"To make things easier for all of us, Björn, we've decided that you're not to go inside this tape. Okay?"

I looked up at his shiny face.

"But how am I supposed to go to the toilet?"

"You'll just have to use the ones on the floor below. The same thing applies to the lift. You'll have to take the stairs to the next floor."

He patted me on the back and went on:

"This will be best for all of us. It's simpler this way."

64.

Håkan wasn't sitting in his place when I got back to our workstation. Just that awful blue jacket tossed over his desk. I sat down and looked round for something to do. I ran my fingers over the pile of files of framework decisions. I picked up the stapler to fasten together the case with reference number 02c11/1, but it wouldn't go through the whole pile and I had to dig the staple out with my fingers.

Even though the paper was designed for being archived, or possibly precisely because of that, it sucked up the moisture from my hands and in one fell swoop lost its smoothness, its purity. A bit of the title page came away with my fingers when I moved them too quickly. The reference number came loose from the framework decision.

65.

I left the Authority just before eleven.

I took my coat, went down the stairs to the floor below, then took the lift from there to reception and rushed out into the sleety snow.

My suit felt sweaty and my shirt was sticking to my body in a very unpleasant way. On top of everything else I felt a sort of pressure across my chest, and I could feel it getting harder and harder to breathe.

When I got to the bottom of the broad flight of steps outside the entrance, I walked straight out into the parking lot and then across the tarmac to the little patch of grass with the sign showing directions to the various departments. I leaned forward and rested my hands on my thighs. I shut my eyes and tried to breathe. There was something that didn't make sense. I couldn't quite put my finger on it, but there was something. Something was terribly wrong. The look on Karl's face, the DG's swift action, his categorical denial—did he really have that level of oversight into every nook and cranny of the building? The makeshift cordon. The whole thing—it felt over the top, somehow. It reminded me of exaggerated, made-up stories designed to conceal something else.

I turned round and walked slowly back toward the building again. This was really just a classic ruling-class tactic, wasn't it? Making someone think they were mentally ill? What was I actually running from?

Down in reception it was as if I was seeing people for the first time. Even the ones I recognized. People I trusted. Now they appeared in an entirely different light. One had an earpiece in his ear. Another ran to catch up with a third. They exchanged a few intense words. The level of activity was stepping up. A black car pulled up and stopped right in front of the entrance. Two men in black coats got out and jogged up the steps and in through the glass doors. Margareta had her eyes on me the whole time, but now it was different. How can I put it? Settled, somehow. As if she understood that I had realized. Could she tell that I had seen through the whole thing? Did she understand that I was about to reveal everything?

The two men in black coats went straight up to Margareta at the desk. It could hardly be a coincidence that all this was happening at this particular moment. This stream of people with an anxious look in their eyes, the new way Margareta was looking at me, the men in the car. It was no accident that they just happened to show up on the day that Karl had been in to see the DG to ask about a room that no one wanted to admit existed.

I got into the lift and pressed the button for the third floor. I realized I still had a small advantage. For the time being they didn't know *who* they were after. The person who had dared to break the pattern and think along new lines. The person who had dared to think "outside the box." But I knew it wouldn't be long before Margareta revealed my identity to them.

I got out on the third floor and went the rest of the way up the stairs. A couple of people stared at me when I entered the department. I slowed down, looked around, tried to seem calm and collected, but when I reached the photocopier I darted quickly round the corner and crept under the barrier toward the room.

Someone cried out. It might have been Ann or Karin. Behind me I could hear Håkan yelling at me to stop. I got the feeling that Jörgen and Karl were somewhere there in the background. When I got to the room I opened the door, then closed and locked it behind me as quickly as I could. For a brief while I could breathe again and think more or less clearly. I leaned against the wall and let my eyes roam round the familiar space. Everything looked much the same, yet somehow different. I could hear the others outside. They were there already, knocking on the door. Banging on the wood. They wouldn't be happy to stay on the outside this time. The blows were getting harder and harder. I realized it was only a matter of time before they forced the door open and got inside and started poking about. I looked round to find somewhere to hide but couldn't see anywhere particularly good. I closed my eyes, took a deep breath, and walked into the wall. The wall closed around me, like yogurt around a spoon.

In there it was dark and soft. Surprisingly clean and free from lines and edges. No angles or corners for dirt to get into and hide. No light. No sound. The smell in there made me think of the sea, and lilacs, and St. Paulsgatan by the junction with Bellmansgatan at five o'clock in the morning at the end of May.

I could hear them calling my name outside, and I thought:

You'll never find me here.

The Room Reading Group Guide

1. What were your first impressions of Björn? Do you think the author intends for us to like him? Is it important to like the protagonist of a story?

2. *The Room* has been compared to the film *Office Space,* NBC's *The Office,* and Joshua Ferris's *Then We Came to the End.* How does *The Room* portray office life?

3. According to Björn, "Inhibited people don't see the world the way it really is. They only see what they themselves want to see." What does Björn perceive that the others don't?

4. Indoor shoes and shoe covers; caviar for breakfast. How did the foreign setting affect your interpretation of the story and characters?

5. Björn makes several references to music and movies during his time alone. What was the effect of these nods to pop culture?

6. From Hannah with the ponytail to Håkan and his shabby blue jacket: Who at the Authority did you relate to? Did you recognize any traits of your own coworkers?

7. Björn comes to feel incredibly alienated from his colleagues. Did you find yourself sympathizing with him? What did you think of the demands he gives Karl in Chapter 58?

8. What do Björn's descriptions of the room (e.g., in Chapters 4, 7, 28, and 36) reveal about his values and needs?

9. How did you respond to Björn's rise to success? What does it suggest about the Authority? About corporate culture in general?

10. *The Room* author Jonas Karlsson is also a playwright and one of Sweden's preeminent actors on screen and stage. Are there elements of *The Room* that remind you of theater or film? How would you stage *The Room* as a play? As a film?

ABOUT THE AUTHOR

Jonas Karlsson, one of Sweden's most prominent actors, has acted in numerous plays at the Royal Dramatic Theatre—Sweden's premier stage—as well as in several highly praised feature films and TV series. In 2005, Karlsson made his debut as a playwright with *Nocturnal Walk* for the Stockholm City Theatre, receiving rave reviews from audience and critics alike. Spurred by the joy of writing for the stage, Karlsson began writing fiction.